Matched in Maple Bay

A Maple Bay Novel

Brittney Joy

Matched in Maple Bay / Brittney Joy; Horse Girl LLC – 1st ed.

ebook ISBN: 978-1-958178-10-2

paperback ISBN: 978-1-958178-12-6

Contents

Never miss a new release ~ Sign-up for Brittney Joy's newsletter:

http://www.brittneyjoybooks.com/newsletter

The Maple Bay Series:
Rescued in Maple Bay
Starting Over in Maple Bay
Second Chance in Maple Bay
Country Stars in Maple Bay
Matched in Maple Bay

Dedicated to my grandparents.
You hold a very special place in my heart.
I hope that one day I have the same, wonderful bond with my own grandbabies.

Chapter One

The glass doors whooshed open, and Valerie Ricci stepped through, exchanging warm sunshine for a chilled office building. The drop in temperature was an immediate reminder of what lay ahead—a boardroom filled with icy stares and jaded network executives.

She took a breath. *My presentation will knock their socks off. I am a rockstar. All my dreams will come true.*

That was the mantra Valerie had been repeating to herself all morning, trying to manifest good vibes. It'd been working . . . until she stepped inside HomeTV's corporate headquarters. The familiar stark-white lobby reignited her nerves, and she suddenly regretted the massive iced coffee she'd guzzled. Her stomach turned. Caffeine and butterflies quarreled in her belly as she remembered the last time she'd been here.

Almost a year ago, Valerie had crossed this same threshold, to be met with devastating news. Her television show—the series

1

she'd put her heart and soul into—had been cancelled. Ratings had slipped, and the network was convinced there was no chance of rebounding. Their decision was the knockout punch she'd been tirelessly fighting.

Especially since the low ratings weren't her fault. *Not exactly.*

But today, Valerie wasn't about to let anyone see her sweat. As she entered the building, her stride didn't hitch.

Shoulders back. Chin up. You got this.

The crisp lines of her shiny black power suit swathed her skin in armor. Her red leather pumps shouted confidence. Her fingers grazed her briefcase, which carried months of preparation. Valerie was ready for battle.

"Valerie!" The receptionist stood and waved from behind the wide u-shaped desk.

"Good Morning, Donna." Valerie strode through the lobby, avoiding stares from curious strangers seated on stiff leather couches. She returned Donna's smile. "I hope you still like Toffee Nut Lattes." She held up the warm drink. "A little birdie told me you'd be working today."

Donna gasped and tugged at the hem of her bright pink blouse. "You are such a gem." Scooting out from behind the desk, she opened her arms and pulled Valerie into a hug. "I'm so glad you're back. The office isn't the same without you."

Valerie embraced Donna with one arm, careful not to spill the latte she balanced in her other hand. "I'm glad to be back." Her response was quieter than she'd intended, though it summed up more than just her visit to HomeTV. It had been a long, hard year for many reasons.

Pulling back from the hug, Valerie offered the warm drink. Donna accepted and immediately sipped. After a delighted sigh and a flutter of lashes, she said, "Nina told me you're pitching to Tom, so I booked the westside boardroom for you. I also ordered in those fancy little cupcakes he likes. The ones with the buttercream swirl." She winked. "Easier to keep his attention with a little sugar."

"You're the best." The tension in Valerie's chest waned. She adjusted the briefcase strap that hung on her shoulder. "I'll take every advantage I can get."

"You'll do fantastic. I know it." Donna patted Valerie on the arm like the mama bear she was. "Besides, how could they say no to you?" At the blind confidence on her face, Valerie's stomach tightened into a knot. Unfortunately, she knew all too well how the network could deny her.

"Hopefully, I'll have good news for you when I come back through the lobby." Running a hand over her blazer's lapel, Valerie tested her armor. Crisp, sleek, and ready to shield her nerves.

"Nina's already in the boardroom. Said to send you up when you arrived." Donna set the latte on the desk and waved over a security guard; a young man Valerie didn't know. "Mick, can you please escort Ms. Star to the westside boardroom?"

Valerie wanted to correct Donna. Instead, she bit her tongue, letting the mistake slide. Star was Valerie's married name, which everyone knew her by. But her marriage was long gone. The star had died, or more accurately exploded, twirling down to the earth in a spray of hot ash. At least Donna led with the correct abbreviation—Ms.

"Sure can," the guard replied, walking over.

Donna handed Valerie a visitor's badge. "Here you go."

"Thank you." Valerie clipped the badge to her blazer, masking the pinch it gave her heart. She had a hard time swallowing the idea of being a guest when she'd been part of this office for years. Ignoring her pride, Valerie smiled at Donna. "Enjoy the latte."

"This way, ma'am," Mick addressed her, and Valerie cringed. She considered telling the guard to call her by her first name. She'd turned forty this year, but that didn't warrant a title she saved for her grandmother. On the way to the seventh floor, Valerie talked lightly about the sunny Los Angeles weather, saving her energy and persuasive skills for the boardroom.

When the elevator dinged and opened, Mick gestured toward the hall. "After you, ma'am."

Valerie stepped out confidently into bright sunshine and a maze of glass. The seventh floor had always reminded her of a fishbowl; every wall was floor to ceiling glass. The architect intended to create an open, collaborative environment, but his execution was poor. The inner workings of every meeting were visible and distracting. Not exactly a functional design for workplace productivity. At least, in her opinion.

Seeing a few former colleagues in a meeting clear on the other side of the building, Valerie politely waved. Then she glanced ahead, spotting her glimmer of sunshine through the transparent walls—Nina Banks.

In the corner conference room, Nina stood, staring out at the hustle and bustle of the city. She wore her version of a power suit—shapeless khakis and a black polo—and Valerie grinned at her friend's blatant disregard of fashion. Nina cared more for comfort than wow factor, at least with clothes. She claimed her creativity was needed on set to produce stunning content, and Valerie couldn't argue with her. Nina was a stellar producer. She'd seen that firsthand during the five seasons of *LA Renovations*—the reality television show Nina had produced and Valerie had starred in.

Mick opened the conference room door, and Valerie stepped through.

"Good morning." Valerie greeted her friend with a singsong, expecting the same excitement in return. But when Nina turned around, Valerie knew something was off. She stilled. "Are you okay?"

The edges of Nina's eyes crinkled. Her dark, curly hair somehow looked less springy. Was she worried? Mad? Sick?

Nina blew out a long breath. "Tom isn't coming for our presentation."

"What?" Valerie's stomach dropped.

Tom Schmitt was the Executive Vice President of Programming for HomeTV. He was the final decision-maker on all new projects. Today, there would be others attending from programming, marketing, and scheduling, but Tom would have final approval. They *needed* Tom to see their presentation and pitch.

"Should we reschedule?" Valerie asked, confused.

Nina shook her head. "He stopped me in the hall when I was heading here." Pursing her lips, Nina paused for an eternity. "He wants to go in a different direction."

Valerie blinked, her stomach turning. "But he hasn't seen our presentation." Valerie and Nina had been working on an idea for a new reality television show for months. Their concept would feature historical buildings across the country, focusing on architecture and design. It was unlike any other program currently on HomeTV. Tom knew the basics of their concept, but they hadn't gone through the details. "We have research and statistics. Vision boards. An outline for a pilot. He doesn't want to see any of that?"

Nina shook her head, looking disappointed. "Said the network can't take a chance on an unproven concept. Not right now. Maybe next year."

"They can't take a chance?" Valerie's voice slid into a high pitch. Didn't the network want something fresh? A show that dove into the history of architecture and design? Wasn't that the cornerstone of HomeTV? Stunned, she pulled a chair from the conference table and set her briefcase on it. "Is it me? Am I the reason he's not interested?"

Tom's dismissal wasn't related to Nina. She still had a job at HomeTV. After the network cancelled LA Renovations, they moved Nina into a producer role for one of the celebrity real estate programs. It was Valerie they'd cast aside, stating that future opportunities would arise. So far, there'd been none, so Valerie was making one for herself.

"No, that's not it." Nina's brown eyes softened. She knew how devastated Valerie was when the show got canceled, but Valerie didn't want pity. She wanted an opportunity to get her hard-earned career back. And to do that, she needed Tom's approval.

Heat bloomed in her chest.

"I know they already offered Ryker another show." Her back straightened when she referred to Ryker Star—her ex-husband and the man she'd co-hosted *LA Renovations* with.

Nina winced. "I just found out. I swear I was going to tell you after our meeting." Stepping forward, she rested her hand on the back of one of the leather chairs at the table. "I didn't want to mess with your head before our presentation. I knew you wouldn't want that either."

Valerie took a breath and nodded. Nina was a straight shooter and wouldn't lie to her.

"I just . . ." Valerie started, pushing down the irritating hurt. "I can't believe Ryker is going to headline his own show, like nothing happened. And Tom can't even show up for our presentation? That's such a double standard. How is it that Ryker can—"

Nina cut her off. "Tom wants you to host a different show. A pilot the network has already approved."

Valerie stuttered, losing her train of thought. She hadn't expected that piece of information. "What?"

"That's why he's not listening to our pitch. Not today anyhow." Nina dropped her hand from the chair. She glanced toward a laptop and spread of papers on the other end of the long table. "He wants you to host the pilot I'm producing."

Valerie tilted her head, knocked off balance. One red heel stepped back, steadying her. "The one you start next week?"

"Yes." Nina nodded, hope coloring her face. "The surprise home makeover show for the sweepstakes winner."

Valerie knew of the project. The network had sponsored a contest in which a lucky winner would receive an all-expenses-paid home makeover. Thousands of people from across the country had submitted videos, telling HomeTV why they needed a home renovation. The marketing department saw the entries as an opportunity to feature the stories, people, and resulting home renovation in a new reality show. It was a brilliant concept. Valerie wasn't supposed to know the details, but Nina could be loose lipped after a sangria or two.

"Isn't Sierra Bishop hosting?" Valerie asked, referring to the actress turned house-flipper who had a reputation of being extremely demanding on set. Nina hadn't been particularly excited to work with her, but the network wanted the social media attention Sierra would bring.

"She was, but she had to *back out*." Nina used finger-quotes around the last two words.

"Back out? Didn't she have a contract?"

Nina put a hand next to her mouth and whispered, "Rehab."

"Oh." Valerie straightened. "Well, I hope she's okay."

"I hope so too," Nina replied. "But we can't wait sixty to ninety days to find out."

Valerie raised her brow, remembering how personal issues could interfere with professional goals. She knew what that was like. Except Sierra hadn't fallen apart *in front* of the camera. Not like Valerie's marriage. "So, production is going to continue without her?"

"Yep. Tom thinks it's too risky to wait. Who knows if Sierra will be okay to do the show, even after she completes rehab? Besides, everything is set for next week. Well, except for a host." Nina stared at Valerie, expectantly. "What do you say? Want to do this with me? I know it's not exactly what you wanted to hear today, but I honestly think this show could be a big hit. And if the network likes the pilot, they'll order more episodes, using other entries from the sweepstakes. You could have another successful series under your belt."

Valerie swallowed, unsure how to feel. She'd been so excited about the concept she and Nina had been working on, but she also knew how Tom was. When he made up his mind, that was it. There was no convincing him otherwise. It was his way or no way at all.

This could be her foot in the door. An opportunity to get back on camera and prove she could headline a show—*without* her ex-husband.

Valerie pursed her lips. Then she gave Nina a lopsided grin. "All right. Where are we going? I need to know what to pack."

Nina's face brightened. "Fabulous!" She clapped her hands together in delight. "We're headed to this adorable town in northern

Minnesota, and the family chosen for the pilot is beyond perfect. They are small-town America at its finest. Sweet as apple pie. The house is this gorgeous Victorian farmhouse. Great bones, but in need of major updates." Nina walked toward the opposite side of the table, toward the laptop and spread of folders. "I've got pictures. You've got to see this."

"A Victorian farmhouse?" Valerie followed, suddenly envisioning carved spindle staircases and flower-patterned wallpaper. She hadn't worked on any Victorian-style homes in LA, but her design skills had been put to test on just about everything else—from boxy modern homes to beach bungalows. And she loved a new challenge.

"The house is next to a lake, and the family has horses." Nina reached the end of the table and opened a folder, exposing photos. "Lots of great opportunities for stunning shots."

Valerie joined Nina and looked over pictures that showed the inside and outside of the home. It looked to be remodeled in the seventies, clear from the avocado appliances occupying the kitchen. "This will make for some great before and after reveals."

"Right?" Nina's excitement spilled through her voice, infecting Valerie as well.

"What's the family's story?" Valerie asked. The house clearly needed fixing up, but there had to be more to the narrative for the network to pick this house out of thousands of entries.

"This family is adorable." Nina shuffled through a few of the photos, pulling out one of a teenage girl and an older woman. Maybe her grandma? They smiled brightly at the camera, arms wrapped around each other's shoulders, looking like the epitome of love. Valerie smiled, the sweetness catching her off guard.

"This is Issy and her grandma, Joyce," Nina said. "They are huge fans of HomeTV, and each wrote an essay explaining the need for a home makeover for Issy's dad, but they have different ideas about why." She chuckled.

Valerie scrunched her brow. "What are their reasons?"

"Issy's essay was about how much she loves her dad and how close they are. Said he raised her as a single parent and she couldn't imagine a better dad. She'll be off to college next year and wants to make sure he's taken care of, because he's always taken care of her." Nina set her hand on her chest. "Doesn't that just melt your heart?"

Valerie nodded, wishing every father and daughter could be so close. Valerie had always wondered what that would've been like. She'd barely known her father until she was an adult and he'd finally grown up enough to attempt a relationship. "And what are the grandma's reasons?"

"Joyce thinks it's about time her son remodels his house so he can land a wife."

Valerie choked on a laugh. "Really?"

"Yes, but she said it in much sweeter words," Nina replied. "Actually, Joyce sounds like a hoot. She also offered her crafting and quilting skills and said she'd feed the entire crew with home-cooked meals and fresh baked pies."

"That's hard to argue with." Joyce sounded like a small-town Martha Stewart.

"But honestly, I can't imagine why Issy's dad would have any trouble finding a wife." Nina shifted the photos around and plucked one from the back of the pile. "Seriously, look at this guy. He'd give Brad Pitt a run for his money."

When Valerie saw the photo, she sucked in a breath, nearly inhaling her entire tongue. Issy's dad was gorgeous in a rugged way—broad shouldered with blue eyes that could bore through steel. But that wasn't what nearly knocked her off her feet. "Is that—?" A hand flew to her heart.

"Val, are you okay?"

"Is that Evan Weston?" Valerie set both hands on the table, steadying herself. Her power suit suddenly felt like a straitjacket.

Nina's expression shifted from worry to confusion. "Uh, yes. That's his name. How'd you know that?"

Valerie pressed her lips together, letting the photo sift through her brain. *Evan Weston.* Her college sweetheart. A man she hadn't spoken to in almost twenty years. The one who had obliterated her heart.

She squeezed her eyes shut. If she agreed to host this pilot—the project that would get her back on camera and possibly put her career back on track—she'd also be signing up to remodel her ex's house.

Instead of explaining her rush of thoughts, Valerie opened her eyes and simply said, "We dated. Back in college."

"Are you serious?" Nina's mouth gaped. "What are the odds of that?"

"Pretty slim, I'd imagine." Valerie didn't think she'd *ever* see Evan again. That had been clear when they broke up.

"Was it a bad breakup?" Nina asked, and Valerie shifted, wondering if her face had projected everything she'd just felt. She stood and took a step back from the table, distancing herself from Evan's photo. *Did any breakup end well?*

"We were young," she replied. "It was a long time ago."

"Will that be a problem?" Nina's eyes narrowed, and Valerie felt picked apart by her friend's sharp gaze.

"No. Not at all." Valerie forced a smile, brushing away the ancient feelings that had jumped up and surprised her. "We're both grown adults. We dated forever ago. Actually, it would be nice to see him again." She lied through her teeth in the last sentence, but they had dated twenty years ago. She was a different person now. Certainly, he was too. This didn't have to be a big deal.

"Okay, good." Nina sighed in relief, moving on to the topic of staffing. Valerie absentmindedly nodded as Nina named off the cinematographer, camera operators, production assistant, and construction crew that would work on the pilot. It was a great team. Valerie had worked with most of them previously and told herself everything would be fine. But when her gaze landed on Evan's photo again, her heart raced nervously, contradicting all positive thoughts.

For a moment, she panicked. If this was her reaction to his picture, what would happen when she saw him in person? And how would Evan react to her?

Yanking her gaze from the photo, Valerie pushed aside her spinning thoughts. She focused on Nina—on what really mattered.

Valerie was not about to let this opportunity pass her by. Another man wouldn't derail her career and ambitions. She'd do this job no matter *who* she had to work with. An ex from forever ago wouldn't stand in her way. Besides, she'd filmed an entire season with her ex-husband while their marriage was in shambles. If she could fake her way through that, she could certainly navigate a week or two with Evan.

Easy peasy. Standing taller, Valerie decided this would be a piece of cake.

Chapter Two

"Sit . . . stay . . . lay down . . . *easy*?" Evan Weston tried every command he could think of, coaxing the six-month-old yellow lab to stay put. So far, nothing had worked. He should've grabbed a kennel from the farm store before leaving. Instead, he'd locked up and rushed out, excited to get home and surprise his daughter with the pup she'd been begging for.

Evan glanced over at his furry passenger. "Good thing it's a short drive home. Having three legs sure doesn't slow you down."

Skippy had been bouncing around Evan's truck cab for the past ten minutes. He now occupied the passenger seat and Evan grasped Skippy's collar, holding the overzealous pup in place while keeping one hand on the wheel.

"You ready to see your new home?" Evan asked. Skippy barked and stared out the windshield like he wanted to be the hood ornament. His tongue hung out the side of his mouth and Evan grinned. "She's going to be so excited."

Issy, Evan's seventeen-year-old daughter, was an animal lover, just like him. Ever since she could walk, she'd brought home creatures to care for. Wounded birds, stray cats, turtles with broken shells. So it didn't surprise Evan when she started volunteering at the local animal rescue, Hooves and Hearts. Issy had been volunteering since she was eleven—and the rescue was also where she'd met the three-legged furball now wiggling around in his truck.

"You know Issy has been begging to adopt you for an entire month?" Evan scratched the pup's neck. "Ever since she laid eyes on you."

Skippy whacked his tail against the seat and Evan shook his head, mostly at himself, for giving in and adopting the pup. It was June, the summer before Issy's senior year of high school. In a year, he'd be moving her off to college and she wouldn't be taking the dog with her. By agreeing to adopt Skippy, Evan was signing on for a solid fifteen years of dog ownership, and it wasn't like he needed another animal. He had five cats and nineteen horses to care for. But he didn't have a dog, and maybe that was what he was missing. A loyal companion, especially when his only child was on the verge of growing up and moving away.

"I think you're really going to like it here." Evan turned onto the long gravel drive toward the white, two-story farmhouse he and Issy called home. But when he looked ahead, it surprised him to see two vehicles parked in front of the garage—Issy's silver Corolla and his parents' truck.

It was just past six o'clock. It wasn't odd to have his parents stop by unannounced, especially since they lived next door—on the opposite side of the horse barn and pastures. But his dad and brother Jesse were feeding the horses tonight. Plus, Evan's mom should be playing bridge with her friends, slinging cards and sipping her second cup of decaf by now.

Maybe they stopped by to drop off goodies? Evan's mom and aunt were always cooking or baking, and he often benefitted from their time in the kitchen.

"Let's see what they're up to. Huh, Skip?" Evan asked, hoping for apple pie or berry cobbler.

Skippy wiggled his rear as Evan parked behind Issy's car. Getting out and walking around the front of the truck, Evan opened the passenger door, careful not to let Skippy launch out. Evan snapped a leash on the pup's collar and lowered him to the ground, getting a few licks in return. Then the pup sniffed and circled as Evan grabbed the warm pizza box from the backseat. He'd stopped at Jake's Restaurant on his way home, grabbing a sausage, olive, and onion pizza—his and Issy's favorite.

"Welcome home, Skip." Evan walked toward the front porch, balancing the pizza box in one hand as Skippy zigzagged, tugging at the leash as he sniffed and romped. As eager as he was, his level of excitement went up a hundred notches when the front door swung open and Issy appeared.

"Skippy?!" Issy screeched and flew out of the house, her long blonde hair trailing behind her.

As soon as she appeared, Skippy turned into a furry cyclone. He spun, barked, and lurched forward, hitting the end of the leash with a force that surprised Evan. The pup couldn't have weighed over fifty pounds. He was equivalent to a bag of horse feed, which Evan threw around all day long at his feed store. He shouldn't have had any trouble controlling Skippy, but Evan had underestimated the power of puppy love.

Knocked off balance by the eager pup, Evan stumbled forward, and the pizza box wobbled in his grip. He quickly released the leash, not wanting grass to become an extra topping, and saved dinner with both hands. When he looked up, Issy and Skippy were rolling on the lawn together in a fit of giggles and dog-kisses. His daughter's laughter instantly brought a smile to his face.

She slung an arm around Skippy's neck and beamed at Evan. "Does this mean he's ours?"

Evan nodded, taking in the beautiful sight. "He's all ours."

There was more laughter and licking. Issy took Skippy's head in her hands and looked him directly in the eyes. "I told you he'd give in, didn't I?"

Evan laughed. "Give in?"

Issy turned her sweet smile back on Evan. "I mean, I told Skippy you'd change your mind and let him join our family."

Evan smirked, knowing his daughter had him wrapped around her little finger. But she was such a good girl. Why shouldn't he give her everything she asked for? Besides, Skippy might keep her from picking a college on the other side of the country. Although she was almost grown, Evan still wanted her to stay close by.

"I thought more about it," Evan said. "And it's about time this family has a dog again." It'd been a year since they'd lost their wonderful golden retriever, Abby, and the house had been quiet without her warm presence.

Issy shot up from the grass and went straight to Evan. She gave him a big hug and a kiss on the cheek. "Thanks, Daddy," she whispered.

His heart melted. "You're welcome. Now, let's get him inside so we can eat some pizza. I'm starving and I've still got to run over to the fairgrounds to get a few things prepped for Maple Bay Days next month."

Issy smirked and hooked her hands behind her back, and Evan suddenly noticed her outfit. She was awfully dressed up for a week-night, wearing pink shorts and a white, flowy tank top. Her long wheat-blonde hair looked to be straightened, and she was wearing makeup.

Evan squinted. "You know the rules about dating."

He'd set rules years ago, long before Issy had her first date. Evan was to meet and interrogate any boy that dared to take his daughter out. Luckily, in a small town, he knew most of the kids. Still, it was his duty to put the fear of God into any boy that thought he deserved Issy's attention.

"I'm not going on a date, Dad." Issy tilted her head, her hair swishing over her shoulder. "But I have a surprise for you." Her face lit up, her hands still behind her back.

"Isabel Joyce Weston, what are you up to?" Just then there was a crash and proceeding yelp that came from inside the house.

Issy spun and stared at the still-open front door. "Uh, oh. Where'd Skippy go?"

Evan was more concerned about *who* had just yelped from inside his house. "Who was that?" It hadn't sounded like either of his parents.

"Come with me." Issy took hold of his arm, leading him onto the porch and into the house. As soon as Evan crossed the threshold, he froze. There were at least ten strangers gathered in his living room. Most were trying to catch a romping, licking Skippy, who had somehow wrapped his leash around a floor lamp and was now dragging it aimlessly.

"What's going on?" Evan asked, though no one heard him. Everyone was jumping about, trying not to get whacked by the lamp or licked by the dog. Someone yelled, "Keep rolling!" Another person shrieked, "Someone grab him!" Two of the strangers balanced big, black cameras on their shoulders. They aimed one camera at Skippy. The other at Evan. The only person he recognized was his mom, Joyce.

"Geez Louise!" Joyce shouted, her hands in the air. "Son of a biscuit! Everyone, hold on to your shorts!"

Skippy raced past the couch and the dragging lamp clotheslined a guy in overalls. It hit him straight in the back of his knees and sent him toppling like dominos. As he fell to the floor, bodies launched at Skippy, and a woman caught the leash. She was crouched down at Skippy's eye-level, which meant she instantly got a face full of sloppy kisses.

"Skippy!" Evan exclaimed as he hastily placed the pizza box on the ground and lurched toward the pup. With a firm grip on

Skippy's collar, he removed the eager dog from the woman, who was shielding her face and holding onto the leash for dear life.

"I got him." Evan tugged the pup close. "You can let go."

Issy knelt next to Evan, putting an arm around Skippy, redirecting the pup's overzealous energy. He licked the side of Issy's face.

"I'm so sorry, Valerie," Issy said. "Are you okay? Is everyone okay?"

It looked as though a tornado had touched down in the living room. The lamp was in two pieces—the base on the floor, the shade on a recliner. The rug was folded up like an accordion, the guy in overalls strewn across it. Someone was helping him up. Everyone else was frozen in various stages of disbelief.

But Evan couldn't look anywhere but at the woman who was still holding the leash.

"Val?" he asked, dumbfounded.

Her wide-eyed gaze connected with his. The silence that followed grabbed him, stilling his heart.

"Hi," she breathed, dropping the leash and pushing her long, dark hair from her face.

"What—" Evan uttered, wondering if this was a practical joke. Valerie Ricci was in his house? His ex? A woman he hadn't seen or spoken to since college? "What's going on?"

Val wiped a string of slobber from her cheek. Her furrowed brow smoothed, and she reached out her hand. Evan numbly took it, thinking she needed help up from the floor. Instead, Val awkwardly shook his hand and smiled politely, like she was greeting a stranger.

"Nice to meet you, Evan," she said from the floor.

His chest twisted. Didn't she recognize him? Trying to shake away the shock, Evan tightened his grip and pulled her to her feet. "What are you doing here?" Maybe she didn't remember him, but he'd never mistake Val. No matter how hard he'd fought to forget her, her memory had never fully faded.

Val straightened and cleared her throat. Instead of answering his question, she brushed down the front of her pressed white shirt. Her olive skin glowed against the crisp fabric. When she looked back at him, her green eyes pierced his soul exactly as he remembered . . . which really freaked him out.

"That might be the most exciting entrance we've ever captured on film," Val addressed the group, giving a dry laugh that scratched him like sandpaper. "Are we still rolling?" She looked over her shoulder. A cameraman nodded. The woman behind him raised a clipboard and gave a thumbs-up. This caused Val to turn back to Evan and flash a bright smile. "Surprise! Your daughter and mother entered you in a HomeTV contest and you won an all-expense-paid home makeover! *Congratulations*!"

Her enthusiasm smacked Evan like a wet towel. "Excuse me?" His gaze shifted to Issy and then to his mom. "This is for a TV show?" Hadn't Val's show been cancelled? After she freaked out on her husband at that fancy restaurant?

Val opened and closed her mouth like a fish, but Evan's mom interjected.

"Isn't that wonderful, Evan?" his mom asked, her hands up. Excitement beamed across her face. "Issy and I entered the contest and now you can remodel your house and all these lovely people are going to help." Joyce waved a hand around the room. Everyone was now standing and staring. At him.

"Remodel my house?" Evan noticed his mom had a fresh perm in her short silver hair. "How long have you two known about this?" He pointed back and forth from Issy to his mom. They were extremely close, practically the same person born a half-century apart. And when they got a scheme in their heads, there was no stopping them. Evan had tried many times.

"Maybe a month." Issy grinned. She was scratching Skippy's head, keeping him distracted. "Isn't it great?!"

Great? Evan had other adjectives he would use. *Unexpected. Unwanted. Uncomfortable and unnecessary.*

"I—" he started, not sure what to say. His living room was full of people and conflicting emotions. Joy was plastered on the faces of Issy and his mom. Val was sporting a weird, fake smile that made him wonder if a robot had replaced her since he's last seen her. The rest of the group looked to be on pins and needles, waiting for him to speak.

How could he get out of this situation?

"We don't need a remodel," he said.

Issy's face dropped. His mom looked as though he'd just announced that her apple pie was average. Val's brow jerked up, but her fake smile stayed.

"What do you mean, Dad?" Issy asked. She'd stopped petting Skippy, and he licked her hand. "You're always saying we need to work on the house, but you never have the time to do it."

"I'll make time." Evan shrugged, brushing off the comment. "After Maple Bay Days. I'll have lots of time then." He wouldn't, but he also didn't need to be on TV, or to accept help from a woman that had left him in the dust during the hardest time of his life.

"Evan," Joyce scolded, breaking his train of thought. "All these nice people came all the way from California and you're just going to send them home? And pass on a *free* home makeover? What in the dickens is wrong with you?"

"I don't think it's a good idea." He scratched his head. "Won't cameras follow us around during the makeover? Then all our business will be on TV for the world to see." He raised a brow, challenging his mother.

"What kind of business are you talking about?" Joyce asked, looking confused. "It's not like you have some skeleton in the closet the world is waiting to uncover."

His skeleton was not in the closet. It was standing right in front of him, and he didn't care to dive back into the tomb.

"Yeah, Dad," Issy chimed in. "It's not like we have any secrets. We live the world's most normal life."

Evan wasn't sure how to take his daughter's comment. There was nothing wrong with their life. It was perfect, just the way it was. They didn't need cameras or a fancy renovation. Would these people fill his house with white furniture and glass chandeliers, like most of the ridiculous mansions Val had worked on?

"I'd like to keep it *normal*," Evan replied. "Besides, I don't need any weirdos watching you on TV and then finding you on social media and sending you creepy messages. I've watched that *Catfish* show. There are plenty of creeps out there."

Issy wrinkled her nose. "Dad, that won't happen."

"It could," he replied, sternly.

"Your personal information won't be shared," Val piped in. She was still standing directly in front of him as though he'd mustered her up from a memory. "We'll only use your first names on the show. The network won't tag any of you on social or mention your full names in the media. You can choose what you'd like to share on your own social. Of course, we will mention the name of the town, so—"

"See." Evan gestured toward Val, but looked at Issy. "This town only has two thousand people in it. Some crazy person could find out who you are if they really wanted to."

"Dad," Issy breathed. This time she spoke his name in the low teenager tone of "you're embarrassing me."

"The show will be on HomeTV." Joyce rested a hand on a hip. "It's a good, wholesome channel watched mainly by ladies of a certain age. It's not like Issy's going on a dating show or something."

"I just don't—" Evan started, but Issy cut in.

"I'm almost eighteen, Dad. I'm not a little girl. I won't get tricked into talking to any creeps. Besides, strange guys already slide into my DMs, even without me being on TV."

Evan was sure his jaw had come unhinged.

"Don't worry," Issy added quickly. "I always block them." Her eyebrows raised like this was obviously the case.

"Ohhhhh—" Joyce strung out the word, giving it multiple syllables. "That *face-place* is the devil."

Issy shook her head, grinning at her grandma. "It's not called face-place, Grandma. It's Face—"

"I think we need a family meeting," Evan interrupted, noting that the cameras were still pointed at them. A long stick arched over the group, nearly grazing the ceiling. A microphone hung from it. "Outside. By ourselves." He glanced at Val. "Excuse us."

"Sure." Val nodded stiffly. "Take your time."

Evan turned and walked out his front door, trying to forget the jolt Val had just given him. He wasn't sure if his pulse was racing from shock, anger, or . . . something else. Why was Val here? Why did she think it was okay to walk back into his life? The least she could've done was reach out to ask for his approval *before* the cameras were rolling. Now the two most important women in his life were intent on participating in Val's show, and it would take some mental gymnastics to change their minds. Though they might think differently if they knew how Val had crushed him.

Evan shook his head, grappling with unwelcome thoughts. Tonight, he'd intended to surprise his daughter with a pup and enjoy a greasy pizza. Instead, a ghost from his past and her camera crew had invaded his house and his life, turning it upside down.

And Evan liked his life right side up, thank you.

Chapter Three

Valerie's stomach flopped to the ground when Evan stalked from the house, Issy and Joyce in tow. She'd expected him to be shocked, but the instant Evan laid eyes on her, a slew of emotions hit his face. Confusion slid into anger, and the news of the renovation seemed to make it worse. He couldn't seriously be upset about winning a home renovation, could he? The irritation had to be aimed at her.

Valerie swallowed. *This is not good.*

"This is pure gold," Nina exclaimed, jerking Valerie from her stupor.

"Huh?" Valerie glanced at Nina. Had she somehow missed the last few minutes?

Nina waggled her clipboard enthusiastically, narrowly missing Valerie's shoulder. "The dog running in like a happy-bulldozer? The sassy grandma? A cute-as-a-button teenager talking about strange guys sliding into her DMs? *Pure. Gold.*" Nina over-enunciated the last two words as if Valerie were hard of hearing. "And let me tell you, Evan is going to give our viewers heart palpitations in all the right ways."

Sasha, the twenty-something production assistant, peered over Nina's shoulder. "Totally. He's mad cute." Sasha's eyes were wide under blunt-cut bangs and Valerie thought her opinion was spot-on. Despite his salty attitude, Evan was made for the camera. Two decades had passed since they'd been in the same room and somehow his good looks had sharpened. How was that possible?

"It's good," Valerie agreed, her jaw tightening. Regardless of Evan's negative reaction, Valerie recognized what was in front of her—a recipe for great television. A sweet family viewers would root for. A gorgeous Victorian home begging for a designer's touch. Beautiful countryside that would pop on screen. It had the potential to be everything Tom had asked for with the pilot.

"Good?" Nina scoffed. "No, this is *great*, and we need more of it. Immediately."

Valerie nodded. "I'll go talk to them." She had to smooth it over with Evan and get him to agree to the show. Pivoting on her heels, she headed toward the front door, motivation renewed. After all, how hard could it be to persuade him to accept a free home makeover? It wasn't like she was asking him to crawl into a vat of snakes or jump out of a plane. But when she stepped outside, Valerie remembered the tough nut she intended to crack.

Across the lawn, Evan stood near his truck, engrossed in a deep discussion with Joyce and Issy. His dusty boots had taken a wide stance in the gravel. He crossed his arms over his chest. If he could've morphed into a brick wall, he would have.

Wow, he really has his panties in a bunch, Valerie thought as she strode across the lawn. *Keep the conversation on track. This is business. All business. And you need to get back to filming. Say whatever it takes to make that happen.*

As she contemplated persuasion tactics, Valerie noticed that Joyce and Issy were dominating the family "discussion." They weren't letting Evan get in a single word, and suddenly Valerie realized that Joyce and Issy were her biggest allies. They were already on her side and wanted to be part of the show. Valerie just needed to add fuel to their fire to pull Evan on board.

As she neared, all three heads turned her way, and Valerie offered a friendly smile, trying to convey warmth and reassurance through her lips and teeth. Joyce and Issy smiled back. Evan's mouth mimicked a ruler.

"I hate to interrupt." Valerie stopped on the edge of the lawn. "I just wanted to reiterate that my crew is extremely professional and will respect any boundaries you'd like to set. We aren't here to cause any issues, and I apologize if we have."

Evan stared stoically, and Valerie continued to ignore the fact that they had history. It was clear that wouldn't help her at this moment. Breaking eye contact with Evan, she aimed an apologetic gaze at Joyce and Issy.

"Oh, you haven't caused any issues, sweetie. We're so glad you and your crew are here." Joyce reached out and patted Valerie's arm. "We were just talking everything over, and I think Evan might have a few more questions for you."

Issy was nodding along as her grandma spoke. Skippy, the three-legged dog, bounced happily beside her like he hadn't just caused pure havoc a few minutes ago.

"Of course." She hoped Evan wanted to ask when they could resume filming and what camera to look at. "What questions can I answer for you?"

Evan's mouth stayed in a straight line. In the awkward silence, Skippy hopped over and licked Valerie's knee, leaving a wet mark on her slacks. She patted him on the head, hoping he wouldn't knock her down and give her a slobber facial again.

"I'm still not sure this is a good idea," Evan said, after Skippy licked Valerie's pants two more times. "And I'm not really keen on—"

Valerie straightened and cut him off when nothing about his words sounded like a question. "I understand you're concerned about having your daughter on television, but Issy is nearly eighteen." She kept her tone even, but she intended to remind Evan that his daughter was practically a legal adult. In another year, she'd be living on her own, without his watchful eye. Heck, she was probably making lots of decisions he didn't know about. Teenagers did that.

Evan's mouth popped open. "I realize that. I just—"

"This could be a very special experience for the two of you. One you'd both remember for the rest of your lives." Valerie took a swing at Evan's heartstrings. He would not be the obstacle that stopped this pilot. Mustering up every sentimental statement she remembered from Issy's and Joyce's essays, she took a breath and continued. "There's a reason you won this home makeover. Both your mom and your daughter poured their hearts out in essays, explaining how much they love you and how much they wanted to give you this gift." Evan's face softened, and Valerie thought she was on the right track. "I know you're a busy man and you've worked very hard to provide a great life for Issy. You're loving and loyal and always put your family first. And I know that because these two ladies made that clear in their essays and video." Valerie waved a hand between Issy and Joyce. They smiled tenderly at Evan, and his shoulders relaxed, though his arms stayed crossed over his chest. Valerie pressed on, jumping to an idea she hoped would pile on the pressure.

"I know Issy is very interested in art and interior design." Valerie focused on Issy. "I was impressed with the pictures you submitted of your artwork and fair projects. You're very talented and really have an eye for composition." Along with her essay, Issy had sent pictures of paintings, pottery, and years' worth of county fair projects ranging from quilts to photography. She'd also noted her interest in pursuing interior design at college next year.

Issy's eyes widened at the praise. "Thank you." She spoke as if she were out of breath, and Valerie immediately took advantage of her reaction. She went in for the kill shot.

"If you'd like, I'd be happy to take you under my wing. You could be my assistant for the week. I'll show you the ins and outs of the design process as we makeover your house."

Issy squeaked and her hand flew to her chest like she might've had a heart attack. "Really?"

"And I'd be happy to write a letter of recommendation after we film the show," Valerie added. "I'm sure that'd help you get into any art program you have your heart set on."

Issy looked faint as Joyce clapped her hands together. "Oh, goodness." Joyce spoke with all the excitement of a proud grandma. "A letter of recommendation from the famous Valerie Star? That would be just marvelous. Wouldn't it, Evan?"

Valerie turned her gaze back to Evan, expecting the slightest bit of appreciation on his face. Instead, his arms had tightened across his chest. It was only when Issy put a hand on his arm that he wavered.

"Come on, Dad," Issy pleaded. "Like I said, I don't have to be on camera if you don't want me to. This will be so much fun and an amazing experience I can put on college applications. Not to mention our house is going to look beautiful. Remember all the gorgeous remodels we saw Valerie do on her last show, *LA Renovations*?"

Valerie's head involuntarily cocked. She blinked at Evan. "You watched my show?" The question formed before her brain could stop it. Pure disbelief had pushed it out. He'd watched her on television? With his daughter?

"A few—" Evan straightened, like she'd caught him cheating on a test. "I caught a few episodes."

"Grandma and I watched your show every Thursday night. It was a standing date," Issy said. "And sometimes Dad would watch too. The demos were his favorite part. Right, Dad?"

Evan cleared his throat. "Issy, why don't you take Skippy inside and see if he's thirsty?" He patted his daughter's hand, which still rested on his forearm. "I need to iron out a few things with Valerie."

Issy smiled tentatively, but followed her dad's suggestion, heading back toward the house with her grandma.

"Can we talk over by the willow tree?" Evan asked Valerie.

"Sure." She nodded and followed Evan to a draping tree behind the house. A wooden swing hung from a high bough. The lake sparkled behind wispy lower branches.

Evan turned toward her, his stare hard enough to cut. "Is this some kind of game?"

"A game?" She jerked back. One of her heels sank into the grass and she shuffled to get a solid stance.

"A publicity stunt or something?"

"What?"

"You can't tell me this was an honest mistake." Evan's blue eyes narrowed, running over her like lasers. "You didn't know it was *me* you were surprising?"

"I didn't know," Valerie retorted. "At least not until a few days ago. I got brought onto this project last minute, and didn't have any involvement in picking the winner for the show." She crossed her arms in front of her, not sure her explanation was helping. "And the premise of the show is to surprise the homeowner. So, *surprise*?" She forced a sheepish grin, even as her insides screamed.

"We can't make our past a part of the show." He swished his hand between his chest and hers, emphasizing his point.

A knot surfaced in her belly, though she wasn't sure why. She wanted that, too. Her personal life did not need to be a topic of conversation in the office or media again.

"I agree," she replied. "Let's keep the past in the past. I don't want to make our history a part of the show at all. In fact, no one on my crew knows we dated." Except Nina. But Valerie swore her to secrecy. "And I want to keep it that way. This is about you and your family. Your home. Your story and renovation. That's it. I'm simply here to design and host. Nothing more."

After a few long beats, Evan nodded. The wrinkles in his forehead eased. "How long will filming take?"

"If we start tomorrow, filming should be done in a week."

"And we can work around my schedule? I still have a feed store to run."

He sure had a lot of demands.

"We want you and your family to take part in the renovation, but we have a team of professionals here to do most of the work. You don't need to be involved in every detail. We can come up with a filming schedule that works for you."

A horse whinnied somewhere off in the distance, and Valerie waited for Evan's answer. She wasn't sure what else would convince him. Next, she'd be resorting to bribery.

"Okay," he said.

Her insides jumped. "Okay? You'll do the show?"

"I'll do the show." He glanced over her shoulder. "Only because it's important to my daughter and mom. We can start filming in the morning, after I feed the horses."

"Great. What time is that?"

"Six-thirty."

Valerie winced, realizing how early she and the crew would need to wake to prepare for filming. Instead of arguing, she said, "Perfect."

Evan gave her a succinct nod. "I'll see you in the morning, then."

He turned, walking back toward Issy and Joyce. When she was out of his stare, Valerie released a heavy breath and let her shoulders sag. She'd gotten what she wanted. Now she had to put on her business-face and focus on the job. She had a week to design and complete a renovation. Seven days to pull together a pilot that would impress Tom. There was no time to dwell on the stubborn cowboy she'd once dated.

Even if his eyes still made her melt.

Chapter Four

Evan was late for filming, but the horses took priority. Pistol, a chestnut colt out of Evan's favorite mare, had somehow unlatched his stall door and roamed freely through the barn overnight. He'd pulled halters off every stall, made a buffet out of the stacked hay bales, and left manure scattered throughout the aisle. Thankfully, he hadn't gotten into anything that had hurt him. This was exactly why Evan locked the feed and tack rooms every night.

"We should've named you Houdini," Evan said to Pistol, letting the horse loose in the grassy pasture. "No more of that funny business, okay?" It wasn't the first time Pistol had escaped overnight. Evan thought the first was a fluke, that someone had accidentally left the stall door unlocked. But two times in a week? "I'll have to add an extra latch to your stall, just in case."

In rebuttal to Evan's suggestion, Pistol raced off into the pasture, giving a hefty buck on his way to join his friends. Evan shook his head at the colt's sass before shutting the gate and jogging to the

UTV. Knowing he needed to make up time, he slid into the driver's seat and cranked the ignition in one motion. The miniature truck whirled to life and Evan sped off around the barn and down the grassy alleyway that split two large pastures. One field was a turnout for the older geldings and mares. The other—which was closest to Evan's house—held broodmares and foals.

Evan whistled as he zoomed by. Two mares lifted their heads from the grass. Their foals were napping and nursing. A few romped like leggy toddlers. For a second, Evan got lost in the peaceful sight, but as he neared the end of the fencing, reality hit him. Beyond the pastures, his usually enticing house looked like a wasp's nest. People buzzed about his lawn, packing cameras and other expensive-looking equipment. Lights were lined up and propped at different angles, all aimed at his front porch where Valerie—the queen bee—stood, speaking to a camera like Miss America.

Evan parked the UTV next to one of the network's vans and killed the engine. A cameraman had turned toward him. Valerie's Miss-America smile faded, and Evan realized he'd interrupted whatever she'd been doing.

"Sorry, I'm late." Evan straightened, pushing his baseball hat further down on his forehead. "Had a horse emergency that couldn't wait."

"No worries." Valerie's smile returned, though it didn't reach her eyes. "We were just filming the introduction for this segment. After this is done, we can start inside."

"That'll give Darla just enough time to get your makeup done!" Nina exclaimed, jerking his attention from Val.

"Makeup?" Evan cocked his head, not sure he heard Nina correctly. "For me?"

"It's just a little powder. Don't worry. Minimizes the shine. We won't pull out the lip liner and blue eyeshadow. Not today anyhow." Nina winked and then yelled "Darla!" with the lungs of a military officer. Evan straightened involuntarily. He was just about to protest when a spry woman with short platinum hair and a black smock jogged around the side of the house.

"Is Mr. Weston finally here?" The excitement on her face was unsettling. Instead of claiming his own name, Evan considered hopping back on the UTV.

"There you are!" She raised both hands. Each contained a fluffy brush, and Evan knew he was in trouble.

"This mug isn't made for makeup." He waved a hand over his face, hoping to keep from getting doused in powder. It wasn't like he'd never worn a smear of makeup. He'd been a single dad since Issy was six years old. She'd used him as her own personal doll many times. One time, he'd nearly scrubbed the skin off his face while removing red lipstick circles from his cheeks.

"Nonsense. Every mug is made for makeup," Darla said, pausing before him and analyzing his face. Evan grinned awkwardly, showing his teeth. "Oh! I see what you mean, Valerie! He has the bone structure of a Greek god and the skin of an angel." She sighed in appreciation, and Evan's gaze jerked to Val.

She'd said *what*?

Val's mouth fell open. "I did *not* call him a Greek god *or* an angel." The words tumbled out of her mouth. Her hands went into balls at her sides.

"Um, okay," Darla replied, thrown by Val's reaction. She shrugged it off and before Evan could contemplate further, Darla grasped the brim of his baseball hat and yanked it from his head. He tried to stop her, but she was quick.

"Oh, yikes. That isn't salvageable." She made a face, emphasizing her words.

Instead of snatching his cap back, Evan ran a hand through his unruly hair, recognizing his bedhead and hat hair. He'd showered late last night and crawled into bed right after. This morning, he'd thrown on his trusty hat on the way out the door well before sunrise.

"I'm overdue for a haircut." He shrugged. Usually, no one cared what his hair looked like, including him. Other than church on Sundays, he always sported a baseball cap or cowboy hat.

"This is true." Darla nodded, evaluating the mess on his head. "I'll take care of that tomorrow." She ran her fingers through the front of his hair, assessing it. Evan felt like a show pony. Was the saddle next?

"He can wear the hat today," Nina interjected. "It's rustic. Gives an authentic country vibe." She turned back to the cameramen, barking out instructions before Evan could tell her it was not a vibe. This was his real life, and he was one-hundred percent pure country.

"Hi, Dad!" Issy's voice sailed through the air. She waved at him from the bay window, her face bursting with excitement. Behind her, a few crew members were moving his couch. His mom was pointing and chatting away.

"Hey, baby." Evan waved back, reminded of why he'd allowed his house to be invaded.

"We're almost ready for you in here." Issy craned her head, looking to Val to make sure she'd also heard.

Val gave Issy a thumbs up. "We'll finish this shot and then we can start inside."

Issy gave two thumbs up.

Evan sighed and looked at Darla. "Okay. Do what you've got to do." He squinted, preparing to be dusted.

Darla pulled a few more resources out of her smock pockets and got to work. She dabbed cream under his eyes and powdered his cheeks and nose. Then she tightened his beard with a trimmer and combed the stubble into place. As she did, Evan observed Val.

On his front porch, Val spoke animatedly at a camera, describing his house as if she were intimately familiar with it. She raved about "great bones" and listed off projects. As she did, Evan absorbed this version of Val. Her dark hair was pulled tight in a bun at the nape of her neck. She wore a white button-down with cream-colored slacks that stopped above bare ankles and high heels. Very high heels.

She looked like a news anchor, or lawyer. When had she gotten so prim and proper? The Val he remembered lived in tattered jeans and comfy sneakers. She didn't care about makeup, but her smile and sparkle could stop traffic. Had she changed that much?

"There you go," Darla said, looking happy with her work. She pulled his hat from her smock pocket and gave it back to him. "All done."

"Thank you." He smiled, knowing she was just doing her job.

"Come thirty minutes early tomorrow and I'll tame those thick, luscious locks for you." Darla winked and headed toward the trailers, which were parked next to the pasture.

Evan shook his head, reminding himself that makeup washed off and hair would grow back. He put his hat on just as Nina called "cut!"

"All right, we're ready to film the demolition inside." Nina clapped. Cameras lowered, and the crew started gathering equipment.

"We're going to take down the wall today?" Evan asked.

Val furrowed her brow in response. "Yes. Just like we talked about yesterday. Are you having second thoughts?"

"No, I like the idea of opening the living room into the kitchen." He gave her a quick once-over, considering her outfit. "I'm just not sure you're appropriately dressed for a demo."

On her last show, Val and her ex-husband were a self-proclaimed "design duo," renovating million-dollar mansions. But as far as Evan could tell, the crew did all the hard work. Val hadn't lifted a finger other than to point at things. Was she planning to sit back and watch while he worked? Point and tell him what to do?

Val tilted her head and gave a dry chuckle, dismissing his suggestion. "We have very capable contractors on staff. I'm not doing the demo."

"That's too bad," he prodded. "I'd like to see you in action." Deciding he was right about her, Evan raised a brow. Just like her outfit, Val had changed. Back in the day, she would have jumped at the chance to get her hands dirty.

"Actually," Nina interrupted, tapping her chin. "That's not a bad idea."

Val shot a wide-eyed look at Nina. A few crew members perked up at the suggestion.

"You want me to take down the wall?" Val asked, as if Nina had lost her marbles.

"Not the entire wall. We'll just get a few shots of you swinging a hammer. That way, we'll have some B-roll footage showing the start of the demo. Then Sal and his crew can finish and work on the archway." Nina seemed way more excited about the idea than Val. "Viewers will eat it up. They'll love seeing you involved, and it'll give you even more credibility as the designer and host."

Her last line seemed to make Val think. She placed a hand on the banister. "You think?"

"Yes," Nina said. "In fact, you and Evan can start the demo together. That'd be a great shot. Come on, let's get to it." Nina strode into the house without waiting for Val to respond. The crew took that as a cue to get moving. They gathered up the rest of the equipment.

Evan meandered to the porch. "You want to borrow some boots? I bet you and Issy are about the same size." He almost felt bad for instigating the idea. Almost.

Val jerked out of her thoughts. "No, thank you."

"You're going to do this in heels?" Had she lost her mind somewhere in California?

Without missing a beat, Val proclaimed, "I can do anything in heels." Then she pivoted and disappeared into his house. Evan took a breath and followed, curiosity urging him forward. This was going to be interesting.

Inside, Issy and his mom were all smiles as the camera crew set up in the now-barren living room. They situated lights on the maroon carpet, which looked older than he remembered. There were dips and rivets where furniture had sat for years. Near the staircase, Evan's dad, Gene, was holding a lively conversation with Sal. They were discussing tractors—which didn't surprise Evan in the least. His dad could go on for hours about machinery. On the opposite side of the room, Val was talking with Nina. Her tone was hushed so Evan couldn't hear her, but it looked like she was trying to wiggle her way out of the demolition.

While everyone prepared, Evan wandered to the wall that was about to come down. It separated the living room from the kitchen, with a doorway on the far side. He ran his hand over the floral wallpaper, which he'd never really liked. But he also put little thought into design or décor. He appreciated comfort and function. And until now, the wall had functioned just fine.

"You ready?" Val sauntered toward him, now sporting a yellow hard hat, safety glasses, and leather gloves. She'd rolled the sleeves of her shirt up to her elbows. Evan almost laughed when she offered him matching gear.

"I'll just take the glasses and gloves. I don't need a helmet." He slid the glasses on his face, but second-guessed his decision when Sal showed up with two hammers. As he slipped on the gloves, Evan wondered about Val's aim.

"It's your head," she warned, and handed the extra helmet off to Sasha, the assistant. "Do with it what you want."

Sal gave Val and Evan each a hammer. "Use two hands, Valerie. A couple of quick whacks should get it started and you can pull the dry wall out with the backend of the hammer or with your hands."

"Thanks, Sal." She gripped the hammer like a baseball bat and narrowed her eyes at the wall.

Oh, boy. This will not end well.

"I can take the first swing and get it started," Evan offered, as he considered backing up.

"Nope. I got it," Val replied. Even through safety glasses, Evan caught the determination in her eyes. He'd forgotten how stubborn she could be. When Val set her mind to something, she did it. He'd witnessed that in her schooling, with her perfect GPA, in every art project she'd immersed herself in. He'd also seen it when she walked away from him. There was no convincing her to stay.

"Okay," he replied, hoping her stubbornness wouldn't cause injury. He took a step back.

Lowering her weapon and straightening her shirt, Val said, "I'm ready."

"All right. Quiet on set," Nina announced, from behind the lighting and cameras. The chatter in the room hushed, and all attention turned to Val and Evan. "Let's capture the start of the demo. Val, why don't you ask Evan a few questions during this scene? Whatever pops into your head. Get conversation flowing. Make it natural. Organic."

Evan cleared his throat. Nothing could be further from organic. There were two cameras and at least ten people staring him down. And now he had to answer questions from Val? He would've preferred to hammer on the wall in silence.

Nina shouted, "Lights, camera, action!" and one cameraman replied with "We're rolling!"

Evan froze, not sure what to do or say. He wasn't an actor. The only speeches he'd ever given were in school and at his brother's wedding. And even then, he'd had notecards to reference. Now they expected him to put on some type of show? His mind went blank, except for his wish to be behind the cameras instead of in front of them.

"I didn't peg you for a floral wallpaper kind of guy," Val said, and Evan's gaze shot to her. The stubborn iciness had melted from her face, replaced with an inviting smile. "I think you're more of a neutral-pallet person. Dark browns. Woodsy, warm tones."

Her words were light, almost flirty. For a second, the change jarred Evan. Then he realized she was charming the cameras. Regardless, the change in energy gave him something to focus on.

"I didn't pick the wallpaper," he replied, not sure he identified with a certain color palette, but green and gold flowers weren't his first choice. "Been meaning to change it since I bought the place."

"Well, we're here to help with that." The film lighting sparkled against Val's pearl-white teeth. "When did you buy your home? It's such a lovely Victorian. So many of the traditional details are still in place."

Evan thrummed his fingers against the hammer handle. This was going to make him sound like a procrastinator—because he'd bought his home a few months before Issy was born. "About . . . eighteen years ago."

"Oh." Val cocked her head. Her eyebrows rose. He expected her to ask why he'd waited so long, but in the next beat, she lightheartedly said, "Well, wallpaper really is a pain to remove, isn't it?"

A huff escaped his throat. "It is."

"But we aren't doing that today." Val presented her hammer. "We're going to take down the wall instead. That's so much easier."

Evan grinned, her comments easing his tight chest. "Not sure about easier, but it'll definitely be faster." He'd helped his parents remove wallpaper from their entryway a few years ago. It had taken an entire weekend and a whole ton of scraping. He raised his hammer, agreeing with her.

"Much faster." Val turned toward the wall. "I think you're really going to like an archway here. It'll open your living room to the kitchen, giving this area more space and light. You'll have lots of room for family gatherings and holiday dinners. How's that sound? Should we start it off?"

Evan paused, Val's on-screen persona drawing him in, taking him to a place and time when she used to look at him like he'd hung the moon. When they couldn't get enough of one another. He'd been trying hard to push those memories to the back of his head, but now they were bleeding through him, flooding his senses with longing and regret. Late-night phone calls that bled into the morning. Weekend meetups that never lasted long enough. A promise for a future together. One that never happened.

He nodded and swallowed, wishing he could remove harsh memories like drywall and old wallpaper. "Let's get started."

Preparing to swing, Val adjusted her helmet, put both hands on the hammer, and took a wide stance on the carpet. Evan squinted, worried about how this would play out, but Val surprised him with a quick, succinct swing and a clean break in the drywall. Still holding tight to the lodged hammer, her mouth parted. Her startled, but gratified smile forced Evan's gaze down her body. He'd done it without thinking, amazed she'd stayed balanced on her ridiculously high heels, but as he took her in, Evan wished he hadn't let his eyes wander. Her white shirt and tailored pants highlighted curves he didn't remember. *Gorgeous, soft curves.*

Evan's traitorous heart bound. He blinked and forced his eyes up—to her face—but her vibrant smile had wobbled.

"Nice swing," he said, trying to forget the irrational pull he felt to her.

Immediately, Val tugged at the hammer and yanked it from the wall. Plaster crumbled and rained to the carpet.

"Thanks," she replied, while staring at the hole. Then, without warning, she took another swing. This one wasn't successful.

The hammer thudded against the wall and bounced from Val's grip. It shot over her shoulder like a thrown axe. Evan barely had time to wince before glass shattered, the room dimmed, and someone screamed. In the same instant, Val staggered sideways.

Instinctively, Evan reached for her, grabbing her shoulder. He'd meant to steady her, but Val toppled like her knees had buckled. Certain she'd fall to the floor, he released his hammer and grabbed Val instead. Swooping in, Evan slid an arm around her waist and pulled her close. She landed against his chest, and he immediately tightened his arms around her. But when she splayed her fingers across his shoulders and looked up at him, his heart lurched like someone had kicked it. A look passed between them, riddled with electricity and unsaid words. Evan forgot about the cameras—until Nina's shrill voice echoed through the room.

"Anyone hurt?" Nina asked.

Immediately, Evan and Val turned their heads to the crew. Thankfully, everyone looked okay. They were startled, but uninjured. The hammer lay at the base of a shattered light.

"I'm so sorry," Val squeaked, and attempted to get her feet underneath her. "No one's hurt, right? I think I found a stud."

Sasha laughed abruptly, and then immediately covered her mouth with a hand. Nina raised an eyebrow, and Valerie froze.

"I hit a stud." Val corrected herself, her green eyes going wide under crooked safety glasses. Evan was still holding her, and she went rigid against him. He loosened his grip. "I hit a stud with my hammer. That's what I meant. I wasn't calling you a stud. I mean, you're handsome, but I wasn't making some demeaning joke or something." She bit her lip, stopping herself, and Evan internally shook away the ache that had just shot through him.

Whatever Val had hit, it didn't want to break. Him included.

"I'm glad no one got hurt," Evan mumbled, and helped Val to her feet. Once she balanced on her hazardous heels, he added, "I think we need to get you some boots."

Chapter Five

"We just got these super cute boots in," Issy said from the backseat of Evan's truck. Her dog Skippy wiggled beside her, hanging on every word. "Square toe. Crepe heel. And they have this gorgeous metallic inlay in the leather. You should definitely try those on."

Valerie smiled at Issy while avoiding eye contact with Evan, who was behind the wheel. His baseball hat shaded his eyes, and dark stubble graced his jaw. It was obvious he didn't want to chauffeur her around. She didn't want it either, but when Valerie had asked where the closest department store was, Issy had insisted Evan take both of them to his farm store. She didn't realize Evan owned the only clothing store within thirty miles.

"Any other recommendations?" Valerie asked, hoping this was going to be a quick trip. She wanted to get some new clothes for the week, head back to the cozy bed-and-breakfast she and the crew were staying at, kick off her heels, and soak in a bath. Currently, she was sweaty, dirty, and uncomfortable. Not to mention, her ankle was throbbing from the tumble she took. She'd twisted it before falling into Evan's arms—which had sent tremors through her heart, stirring emotions she hadn't expected.

"Do you have any Wranglers?" Issy asked, scratching Skippy's ears.

Valerie chuckled, but quickly realized Issy wasn't kidding. "Uh. No, I don't." She glanced down at her white shirt and tan slacks, which were now covered in drywall dust. "I'll need some jeans and a few tops."

"We'll be there in just a few minutes," Evan said, one hand on the steering wheel. His opposite arm rested on the console between them. He was covered in just as much filth as she was. Maybe more. But somehow it looked good on him. *Masculine. Rugged.* Like a badge of honor.

Evan glanced in the rearview mirror at Issy. "You should show Val the Carhartt shirts."

Valerie stared at Evan, unsure how to feel about her nickname. No one shortened her name anymore, but it easily rolled off Evan's tongue, making her warm and uncomfortable at the same time.

"Yeah, those shirts are super durable and come in tons of colors." Issy tapped her finger to her chin, thinking. "Once we get to the store, I'll show you all my favorite things."

"That'd be great. Thank you." Valerie glanced outside, scanning the corn fields and farmhouses. If she was going to be physically involved in this renovation, she'd need a new wardrobe. Her suitcase was full of designer clothing and pretty heels. She'd packed tennis shoes and sweatpants to lounge in, but she certainly couldn't wear those on camera. This shopping trip might not be as quick as she wanted it to be.

On *LA Renovations*, she'd been the designer and creative force. That was her role and forte. She took care of the layout, color palettes, textiles, and décor—all the planning and pieces that made a home. The physical labor was her ex-husband's responsibility, but even Ryker hadn't taken part in much of the actual work. He'd directed the staff and charmed the camera. But if Nina thought Valerie should be more "hands-on" for the pilot, then Valerie would eagerly swing hammers, paint walls, and even run a saw. She wanted the network to recognize the potential in a series and would go to great lengths to make that happen. However, she needed to ditch the high heels and tight slacks to do so. Today, she'd nearly broken her ankle. She'd also ended up in Evan's arms, breathless and way too close to his tempting mouth.

Valerie straightened against the seatback, tingles rolling through her belly. *Not good.* She did not need to be that close to Evan. Especially on camera. Who knows what her face had conveyed in that moment? Her heart had just about beat out of her chest when she slammed into him, not expecting the fall or the rush of adrenaline that came with his strong embrace. Valerie had attributed her body's ridiculous response to the incident itself—the flying hammer and broken glass. But even now, Valerie's pulse snapped as she remembered the way his eyes had locked onto hers.

"How long have you owned the store?" Valerie asked, drumming her fingers against her thigh, searching for conversation to redirect her brain. What was she thinking? She had no reason to fixate on anything Evan-related, other than his house.

"Almost ten years." Evan slowed the truck and turned into a gravel lot. He parked next to a row of trucks. "I got tired of driving an hour to Elm Grove to pick up feed for the horses, so I opened a farm store closer to home."

"Oh," she replied, thinking his simple explanation contradicted the beauty before her. This was his farm store?

A big red barn edged the gravel lot, looking like a magazine spread. The tall gambrel roof framed the structure against blue sky. A covered porch, adorned with potted flowers and charming bistro sets, wrapped around the front and sides. A couple sat at one table, enjoying ice cream cones.

Evan opened his door and got out. Valerie followed, nearly tripping on gravel as she took in more of the barn's architectural details. Stone columns anchored the porch. Antique lanterns framed the open double door, and as Valerie entered, the inside was just as adorable as the outside.

"Wow," Valerie muttered to herself. The lofted ceiling exposed thick wood beams. Tall windows doused the store in sunshine and there were plenty of customers milling about, shopping through racks of jeans and cowboy hats. The backside of the building looked to be filled with pallets of feed bags and there was even an old-fashioned ice cream parlor in the corner.

Stunned, Valerie paused near an antiqued buffet filled with candles, lotions, and knickknacks. She turned to Evan. "This is your store?"

His eyes crinkled at the edges, like she'd just discovered his secret. "Welcome to Weston Feed and Seed."

Just then, Issy and Skippy romped over. "Let's start with the jeans first," Issy said, taking Valerie by the arm.

Valerie had a lot of questions for Evan, but Issy tugged Valerie into the women's clothing section and bombarded Valerie with questions of her own. *What are your favorite colors? Do you need a belt? How do you feel about overalls?* As Valerie answered, Issy plucked clothing from racks and tables. Soon, Valerie had an armful of options and Issy showed her to a fitting room, bringing her different sizes as needed.

"You know, you're really good at this," Valerie admitted, as Issy tossed another tank top over the top of the fitting room door.

"I should be," Issy replied lightheartedly. "I've been helping Dad with the store since I was eight. He even lets me place orders now. I picked out most of the stuff you've got in the fitting room."

"You've got good taste." Valerie slid the tank top on. It was a pale violet color, snug across her chest, but flowy over her stomach and hips. Cotton, breathable, and cute. The color contrasted perfectly with the dark denim Wranglers she wore. And the cowboy boots on her feet were actually comfortable. She gave herself a once over in the full-length mirror, cocking a leg. *I look like a different person.* Or, at least, not like the person she'd been in the past decade.

"I think I'm good on jeans and tops now," Valerie said to Issy. "Do you want to show me those other boots you were telling me about?" While she was here, she might as well get a couple of pairs.

When Issy didn't reply, Valerie opened the door, but her heart skidded to a halt when she found Evan. He was holding a boot box under one arm and saying something to Issy as she jogged toward the back of the store.

"She's going to help—" Evan started, turning to Valerie. When his gaze landed on her, his mouth stopped. Suddenly, Valerie wasn't sure how she felt in her new attire. She pressed her hands against her thighs. She probably looked like a city girl dressing up as a cowgirl for Halloween.

"What do you think?" she asked, not sure she wanted his answer.

"You look beautiful." The words left his lips quickly, catching Valerie off guard.

"I, uh—" *Beautiful?* Valerie's stomach did a flip flop. She pushed a loose strand of hair from her face, now extra aware that her bun was halfway undone, and she'd sweated away most of her makeup. "I mean, do you think this is more appropriate for the renovation?"

Evan cleared his throat with a quick shake of his head. "That'll be perfect." His blue eyes came back to her, his stare prompting memories to bubble up.

"Great." She swiped at the strand of hair she'd already pushed behind her ear. How was it that this man could still make her nervous? She wasn't twenty-one anymore, but the way he'd looked at her when she'd fallen into his arms . . . how he was looking at her now . . . it made her knees wobble. "Are those the other boots Issy wanted me to try on?" She glanced at the boot box tucked under his arm, avoiding the emotions firing inside her.

"Yeah." He walked to the bench where her high heels and purse laid. "Issy has a few friends here to pick up feed. She's helping them load it into their truck and then she'll be back. She asked me to give you these."

"Oh, okay. Thanks." Valerie tentatively followed Evan and sat on the bench. As she plucked a brown boot from her foot, Evan opened the box, exposing the fancy boots Issy had been gushing about. They were black with a floral design that ran up the tall tops. "Wow, they're gorgeous," Valerie said, feeling like a cowgirl Cinderella. Immediately, she added, "If you've got other things to do, that's fine. I got this." She didn't want him to feel like he had to stay with her.

"I've got everything taken care of for today." Evan pulled one of the fancy boots from the box and removed the filler from inside. "I've got great employees and they're holding down the fort. At least so far. I guess we're only on day one of filming, but no major catastrophes yet."

"That's good," she replied. "Are you here most days?"

"Most days, but we're closed on Sundays. All the businesses around here are."

"Nice to have a day off."

Evan chuckled, grabbing the second boot. "Not sure I'd call it a day off. I usually catch up on payroll and orders during any downtime, outside of church and family supper. Honestly, there aren't enough hours in the day."

Valerie stared at him for a moment, a pang of understanding grabbing her. Maybe Evan had turned into a workaholic, just like her? As she contemplated this, she yanked the other boot from her foot, but winced at the sharp pain that shot through her ankle. Valerie sucked in a breath, and Evan's gaze snapped to hers.

"You okay?" he asked, the lid of the boot box falling shut.

Setting her ankle on her knee, she rubbed her own socked foot. "I'm fine." Her toes screamed from the heels she'd worn all day and her ankle was throbbing, but it wasn't anything a few Advil couldn't handle. "My ankle's just a little sore."

His brow furrowed. "From your tumble?"

"Yeah," she uttered, not wanting to admit her stubborn streak had overruled common sense. "I rolled my ankle, but it's nothing major." Tensing, she braced herself for a lecture about wearing appropriate footwear. Instead, Evan knelt beside her and gently grasped her foot. Before she knew it, he was inching down her sock.

"Can I take a look?" He looked up at her, seeking permission. The tenderness of his gesture snatched the breath from her lungs.

Her back straightened. Suddenly, she didn't know what to do with her hands. Awkwardly, she gathered them in her lap. "Uh, sure."

Focusing back on her ankle, Evan gently tugged her sock down and off. His fingers grazed her skin and a rush of warmth spread through her like a gulp of hot tea. Momentarily, she forgot about the pain, and bit her bottom lip, holding back an embarrassing gasp.

"Does that hurt?" He analyzed her ankle, rolling his hand over bare skin. A shiver spread up her leg and back.

"No, it's fine. Really." Valerie bit her lip harder.

"It looks swollen. You should put your feet up tonight and put some ice on it."

His gaze rose to hers, and Valerie wasn't sure what to do. When was the last time someone had fussed over her? She took care of herself—in all aspects of her life. She'd nearly forgotten how it felt to be doted on. To have a man get on a knee and . . .

Her chest seized up like she'd been caught in a vise.

With Evan kneeling, Valerie suddenly remembered the last time she'd seen him in that position—staring at her with love in his eyes as he proposed. Elation and sadness hit her with such force that she tugged her foot from him and forced it to the ground. The memory was too much.

"I'll put my feet up tonight," she said, ignoring her throbbing ankle and the new tension between her and Evan.

Evan pressed his lips together and rested an arm on his knee. He opened his mouth as if he had something to say.

No. We're not talking about this. A rock lodged in her throat. She wasn't ready to revisit their engagement and the heartbreak that followed. Was she?

When Valerie's phone rang, she was immediately grateful for the interruption. She grabbed her purse and pulled it close. "Thanks for looking at my ankle." Digging into her purse, she searched for the ringing phone. "I'll ice it." When she found the vibrating device, she yanked it from the clutter, relieved to see it was her sister calling.

"Excuse me," Valerie said. "I need to take this." She would've answered a telemarketer in that moment.

Evan stood, his expression unreadable. "Okay," he breathed.

Valerie nodded, avoiding his gaze. The past was in the past, and she couldn't let it derail her future.

Chapter Six

Evan absently pushed a wheelbarrow brimming with hay down the barn aisle, tossing dinner to the eager horses in their stalls. But his mind was elsewhere, consumed by the events of the day. Lost in thought, he hardly noticed the nickers and stomps from the animals demanding their dinner. It wasn't until his brother Jesse strode past him with a horse that Evan was abruptly jolted back to reality.

"You hear what I said about that stallion?" Jesse asked, leading his horse, Indy, into a stall.

"Huh?" Evan asked. Had Jesse been talking to him?

"I said we should look at that new stallion at Lone River Ranch." Jesse removed Indy's halter and scratched him on the forehead. The buckskin gelding blinked his eyes lovingly. "He's sired some good-looking colts in the past few years. He's quick and cowy. I think he'd be a great match for a few of our broodmares next year."

"Sounds good," Evan responded, his thoughts moving to the hungry horses in front of him. One impatient filly was sticking her neck out of her stall, giving Evan a pointed look that made it clear she expected to be fed immediately. Her persistent head-bobbing only stopped when Evan threw her some hay.

Jesse closed Indy's stall door. "You're awfully quiet tonight," he observed, hanging the halter on a hook and giving Evan a curious look. "Has it got something to do with the fact that you've been spending time with your ex-fiancé?"

Evan shook his head, not wanting to talk about the subject, even though Val had been the focus of his thoughts ever since she'd stepped back into his life.

"I'd like to keep that between you and me. The ex-fiancé part." Evan glanced over his shoulder, making sure no one else was in earshot. Thankfully, Issy was on the other end of the barn, handing out carrots to the broodmares. Evan's dad walked beside her, chatting away. "You didn't say anything to Hazel, did you?"

Jesse shook his head, stepping closer. "I haven't said a peep to my wife, but if she finds out I'm keeping a secret from her." He gave a low whistle. "I'm definitely putting all the blame on you."

"I'll take the blame," Evan replied, hoping that would be the end of it. After all, Val wasn't interested in broadcasting their history, either. Evan held his brother's gaze until Jesse finally relented with a sigh.

"Hey, it's your funeral." Jesse plucked hay out of the wheelbarrow and plopped it into Indy's stall. "Mom might not talk to you for the rest of the year if she finds out you were once engaged to her favorite TV star, and you never told her."

"She wasn't on TV back then."

Jesse tipped his head at Evan. "You think that's the part she's going to care about?"

Evan pushed the wheelbarrow past his brother, knowing Jesse was right but not wanting to admit it.

Evan hadn't kept his relationship with Val a secret from his family. His senior year of college, they knew he had a long-distance girlfriend. Evan had been playing football at the University of Minnesota. Val attended the University of Nebraska, getting her Bachelors of Art. They'd crossed paths when Evan was in Nebraska for an away-game, and the sassy, quirky art student had immediately captured his heart. Their chance-meeting at a local café had quickly spiraled into an intense romance. It had been the first time Evan had truly fallen in love, and he thought they'd be together forever.

During their relationship, Jesse was the only family member Val had met in person. Evan had also only confided in Jesse about their brief engagement. After Val left him, Evan couldn't bring himself to tell the rest of his family about the proposal. He'd felt embarrassed that someone he loved so deeply had accepted his proposal, only to change her mind a few days later. Instead, he told his family that he and Val had gone their separate ways, knowing they weren't right for each other.

Years later, when Val appeared on his mom's favorite TV channel, Evan didn't see the point of telling anyone about their past. By then he was married with a daughter, and Val had a different last name. Bringing up his previous relationship with Val would only cause unnecessary commotion.

"Let's leave the past in the past. Okay?" Evan said, feeding the last horse. "I don't want to make a big deal out of it and upset Mom."

"I won't say anything." Jesse raised his hand, giving the Boy Scout's honor. "But good luck in making it through the week without the women in this family figuring out the connection between you and Val." Jesse gave Evan a look of pity. "They're like a pack of female Sherlock Holmes."

With a heavy sigh, Evan pushed the empty wheelbarrow to the bay stacked with hay bales. He grabbed a bale and set it in the wheelbarrow, reminding himself that Val was only here for a short time. Soon she'd return to California, and he hoped that once she was gone, he could finally stop thinking about her. But he'd tried to convince himself of that before, and it had never worked. Val had a way of staying in his head and heart, no matter how hard he tried to forget her.

The next morning, Evan rose well before the sun was up. He and Issy were staying at his parents' house for the duration of the remodel, and while that displaced him a bit, it wasn't a hardship to stay with his mom and dad. First, it put him even closer to the horses, as the stables were in his parents' backyard. Second, he could count on being well fed for the week. In fact, by the time he got dressed and downstairs, a hot pot of coffee was waiting and a pan of cinnamon rolls plumped in the oven. Getting comfortable at the table, he enjoyed a sweet breakfast with his parents before filling a thermos of coffee to go.

"I've got to stop over at the store this morning. Meet you guys at my house?" Evan asked, walking toward the back door. His sister Kat and her husband Creed were feeding the horses this morning, but Evan had office work to catch up on.

"Sure thing, sweetie," his mom replied. "Nina said to be there at eight."

His dad raised his coffee mug in agreement.

"I'll see you over there. Thanks for breakfast." Evan patted his full stomach—which made his mom grin—and headed out the door.

After getting paperwork done at the store, Evan arrived at his house a few minutes before eight. Darla promptly swept him off, leading him to a trailer where she plopped him in a chair and fussed on him for far too long—in Evan's opinion. After a haircut, beard trim, and dusting of makeup, Darla deemed him "prettied up for the cameras" and sent him on his way.

Sasha took it from there, escorting him back to the house. "They started filming," she explained, clipboard in hand. "But they should be ready for you to come on camera now."

"Okay." Evan said, cautiously. "What project are we working on today?"

"If I told you that, we won't get your genuine reaction on film."
Sasha gave a mischievous smile, and Evan suddenly wondered what
was transpiring in his house. Before he could think too much
about it, they reached the front door. "Go on in. They're expecting
you. I'll stay on the porch." She clenched the clipboard to her
chest.

As Evan opened the door, he braced himself for what he might
find inside. With one foot over the threshold, he paused, startled
by the sight before him. The entire first floor of his house was
visible from the doorway. The wall that had separated the living
room from the kitchen was gone, leaving an unobstructed view
straight to the cupboards and fridge. The drop ceiling was partially
dismantled, with a heap of vinyl tiles near the back door. And
the carpet in the living room had been ripped up and rolled back,
revealing the dusty floor underneath.

"Whoa," Evan murmured, frozen in place. The clatter of construction dwindled. Val stood from where she'd been crouched,
near the torn-up carpet.

"What do you think?" Her face was bright, smiling like she'd
found a treasure.

"I, uh—" Evan stuttered, aware a camera was on him. He
stopped himself from saying the first thing that came to mind:
You're ripping apart my entire house.

"Isn't it amazing?" his mom called from behind Val. She stood
near a folding table that held a pan of cinnamon rolls. A few
workers circled her. "You guys are doing such a wonderful job."

Scooping a roll onto a paper plate, she handed it to Sal. He was practically drooling.

"After this, we have a few projects for you guys at our place," Evan's dad said from the kitchen with a chuckle. He was monitoring the deconstruction of the ceiling.

"Who else wants a roll?" His mom asked, ignoring Evan's stunned silence. Her question stopped the construction. Tools jangled as they were set down, and the crew headed straight for the folding table.

Val's smile wavered. "You don't like it?" she asked. The cameras stayed focused on her and Evan.

"It's—" Evan paused, running a hand through his freshly cut hair. "It's . . . a lot different."

"It's what we talked about." Confusion seeped onto her face.

"You said you were going to open up the space," he started. "But I didn't expect all of this." Remembering the remodels that Val and her husband had done on LA Renovations, Evan stiffened. There had been a lot of chandeliers and wine cellars. In one house, they'd added a waterfall to an entryway. He should've asked a few more questions before giving her the go-ahead. His house needed updates, but it had always worked just fine for him and Issy. They didn't need anything fancy. Was Valerie treating his home like one of her over-the-top Hollywood renovations?

"I don't need a waterfall in my living room," Evan blurted. "Or appliances smarter than me."

Val's forehead scrunched. "I wasn't planning on any of that."

"I just want to keep things simple. *Comfortable.*" Now Evan wondered if he could put his house back together.

"That's what we're doing." There was an edge to her statement.

Evan glanced at the destruction. "This doesn't look simple."

Val set a hand on her hip. Then, with a tilt of her head, she said, "You can't see it."

"Can't see it?" He could clearly see what was happening to his house.

"I mean, you can't picture the end result." Val dropped her hand from her hip. She navigated around the ripped-up carpet and grabbed a briefcase perched on the staircase. "Most people can't. It's hard to see with an untrained eye."

Evan bristled at her implication that he couldn't understand the renovation process. He didn't need formal training or degrees to know what he wanted. Val was used to working with fancy clients in the city, while he preferred a more rustic style. Their tastes were completely different.

"I think we should pause and take a step back," he suggested, catching his mother's attention. "Re-evaluate."

"Here. This might clarify things." Val pulled a laptop from the briefcase. She flipped it open and walked toward Evan. "Can I show you the renderings?"

He steeled himself, ready to hold his ground, but when Val stood beside him, the design on her laptop screen was not what he'd expected.

"I wanted to bring out the history of your house, but also combine it with your style." Val tilted the screen back to give Evan a good view. "Make it practical and comfortable while preserving the original features of your home."

The fight in Evan fizzled as he absorbed the rendering. It was a three-dimensional image showing the remodeled first floor of his house. He closed his mouth, taking in the entirety of Val's design.

She scooted closer. "The new archway between the living room and kitchen will be lined in maple trim, to match your new kitchen cabinets and island." Her finger twirled around the laptop screen like a wand. "We're going to refinish the staircase and all the wood floors that have been hiding beneath the carpet. We'll fix the brick fireplace so you can actually use it in the winter. Sal is also going to add a hearth and mantel."

Evan's gaze jumped from the computer to his deconstructed house and back again. "You're going to do *this*?" He pointed to the rendering. The image was so realistic that it felt like he was standing in the renovated space. And it was nothing like the over-the-top designs Val was known for. The design was cozy and inviting. Soft white hues on the walls. A butcher block island surrounded by stools. The appliances blended with the rest of the design—not flashy or gratuitous. Overall, the space felt warm, welcoming, and practical, yet elegant and timeless. Evan was impressed, feeling a glimmer of excitement as he pictured family dinners in the open kitchen, cowboy boots lined up by the back door, and chilly mornings warmed by a roaring fire.

"What did you think I was going to do?" Val asked.

He looked at her. Her black hair was pulled into a tight bun again, but today she wore dark Wranglers and the same flowy tank top she'd modeled for him at the feed store. The one that had put a hitch in his breath and reminded him of who she used to be.

"I—" He paused, embarrassed. "I didn't expect this."

"Do you like it?"

"I do." He loved it.

"Good." Val's smile returned. "I had a different plan for this space, but after going to your store, I got a better idea of your style. I was up late last night recreating the renderings. This design is a mix of old and new. I'd call it a blend of Victorian, contemporary, and farmhouse chic."

He blinked at her, amazed at how she'd created something he hadn't even known he wanted.

"I like the blend of old and new," he admitted. "I guess I thought you were going to rip out everything and start from scratch."

Val gasped and shook her head. "Goodness, no. I want to bring beauty back to the original features. There's over a century of history here and that deserves to be preserved, not torn down and discarded." Her words were infused with passion, which moved Evan's thoughts beyond the renovation to his history. *Their* history.

His gaze flicked to Val, certain she hadn't been referring to anything deeper than wood floors or banisters, but she was staring into the distance. Was she looking at the kitchen? The cinnamon rolls? For a moment, Evan wondered if she'd fallen back in time as well. Then she gave him a tight smile and closed the laptop, tucking it under her arm.

"I'm glad you like it." Ending their conversation, Val walked off, leaving Evan with questions he hadn't pondered in years.

Were there still feelings there? Was it possible that a devastating heartbreak and two decades of distance still hadn't erased their connection?

Chapter Seven

A soft melody floated out from the vintage radio while Valerie untangled her damp hair with a brush. As she worked through a stubborn knot, her gaze drifted around the cozy room she rented for the week at The Carriage House Bed and Breakfast. The walls were a soothing shade of sage green, highlighting dark wooden rafters on the slanted ceiling. In the center of the room, a magnificent four-poster bed stood proudly, adorned with a colorful patchwork quilt and an array of fluffy pillows. In the corner, a deep clawfoot bathtub had just finished draining, leaving behind a trail of bubbles.

"I need to do that more often," she told herself, as the bathtub glugged. Setting her brush on the sink, Valerie considered redesigning her condo bathroom back in LA. It had a huge double shower with white marble she'd painstakingly handpicked, but Valerie had almost forgotten what a hot bubble bath could do. It forced her to relax.

Stepping over to the tub, she ran her fingers over the curled ivory edge. "I'll make good use of you while I'm here." Besides, if the network signed her on for more episodes beyond this pilot, she'd be on the road for the foreseeable future—filming and renovating. No need to think about remodeling her condo right now.

"But I could use a cup of tea," she decided, rotating her foot. "And ice for this ankle." Being on her feet all day had brought the swelling back.

After throwing on her favorite pajamas—a tattered pair of cutoff sweatpants and a t-shirt so worn that it felt like a second skin—Valerie clicked off the radio and opened the bedroom door, surveying her surroundings before stepping out.

Her room was on the second floor of the inn, in what used to be a hayloft half a century ago when the building had been a real carriage house. That's what the owner—Hazel Weston—had told Valerie when she'd first checked in. The rest of the loft had been converted into a cozy space where breakfast was served each morning. The far corner held a full kitchen, which framed a long wooden table. But her favorite piece of furniture was the L-shaped couch that faced the backside of the carriage house—and the wall of windows with a view of the lake.

Padding toward the windows with bare feet, Valerie took a moment to enjoy the sight. Maple Leaf Lake wasn't more than a few hundred feet from the inn, and the sun was setting over its dark, glassy waters. Bands of gold and peach wrapped the tips of trees, and Valerie crossed her arms over her chest, absorbing the sight.

"Pretty sunset, isn't it?" The deep voice startled her, and Valerie whirled around, finding Evan standing in the open doorway that led downstairs.

"Goodness." She pressed a hand to her thumping heart.

"Didn't mean to scare you." He raised his arms, showing off two full grocery bags. "Hazel and Jesse are having a hard time getting the baby to sleep, so I offered to drop off supplies for the morning." He stepped toward the kitchen and set the bags on the counter.

Valerie stood frozen, wondering if it was too late to make a run for it and hide in her room. Suddenly, she felt naked and vulnerable, standing there in ratty pajamas, wet hair, and no makeup. Her arms locked across her chest. "I was just going to make some tea." She didn't think she'd run into anyone. Especially not Evan.

"Tea?" He pulled a bottle of orange juice from one of the paper bags and opened the fridge to slide it onto a shelf.

"Yes," she replied, wondering how quickly she could make a cup. Or maybe she should go to her room and come back after Evan had put away groceries. He'd seen her in pajamas many times, but now it felt as if there weren't enough layers between them.

He glanced at her while pulling a few bunches of bananas from the bag. "Your ankle still bothering you?" He set the bananas in a fruit bowl, and Valerie realized she had one leg cocked, taking the pressure off her swollen ankle.

"A little." She straightened her leg, ignoring the dull, annoying throb.

Evan opened a drawer, removed a dish towel, and stepped over to the freezer. "I'll get you some peas."

Peas? Before she could question how the conversation had turned to vegetables, Evan was walking toward her with a bag of frozen peas.

"Hazel keeps a few bags in the freezer. Her sister has three active little boys who get a few bumps and bruises." He wrapped the bag in the dish towel and offered it to her. "It's a lot more comfortable than a bag of ice cubes."

"Oh," she replied, every muscle cinching. With Evan standing just a few feet in front of her, Valerie couldn't help but feel exposed. She was used to being done-up, relying on makeup and tailored clothes to hide insecurities. But in that moment, her bare face, wet hair, and curves were on full display, and she couldn't help but feel self-conscious. She'd gained a few pounds and wrinkles since the last time Evan had seen her.

Evan held the bag out, waiting for her to take it. "You need to keep the swelling down so you can heal faster. Why don't you sit down and ice your ankle? I'll make you some tea."

"I can make my tea," she said, trying to hurry him along.

"I'm sure you can." He nudged the peas at her, looking her straight in the eye. "But you're a guest at The Carriage House. Hazel would have my head if she found out I was here and let you make your own tea. Especially while you're recovering from a *high-heel injury*." He smirked. "Take the peas, Val. Please."

She wanted to say no, but Evan cocked his head and the warm tones of the sunset washed over his face, highlighting chiseled features and freshly cut hair. Valerie took hold of the frozen vegetables, mainly to focus on something other than his handsome face.

How was it she was fighting wrinkles and sunspots with a million creams and lotions, but somehow Evan had aged like fine wine?

"Thank you," she replied, truly appreciating the gesture even though she'd fought it. "But please refer to my swollen ankle as a workplace accident."

He smiled, looking satisfied at her jest. "I like the sound of *high-heel injury* much better."

A soft laugh escaped her. The tension between them eased, and Evan headed back to the kitchen. As he filled a teapot with water, Valerie retreated to the L-shaped couch. She nestled into the corner and situated the towel-wrapped vegetables on her ankle. They conformed like a cold bean bag, and Valerie agreed the peas were much more comfortable than the bag of hard ice cubes she'd used last night.

Evan set the teapot on the stove and dug back into the groceries.

"I really do like what you're doing with my house." He reached up, adding a few loaves of bread to a cupboard. "I know I've been stubborn about the whole thing, but I like how it's coming together."

He continued putting supplies away, and Valerie wondered if this was an olive branch. His way of soothing the tension between them. She carefully took the bait.

"I'm glad you liked it after you saw the renderings." She tugged a throw blanket from the back of the couch onto her lap, feeling more at ease with her legs covered.

"I guess I was worried you were going to fill my house with crystal chandeliers or something." He glanced over his shoulder at her.

"Crystal chandeliers? Yuck." When was the last time she'd put one of those in a house? "That doesn't fit your style."

"And how would you describe my style?" Evan asked, putting more food in the fridge.

Valerie drummed her fingers on her knee, considering how to sum up Evan's taste. "Country boy meets old soul."

Evan closed the fridge, keeping his hand on the handle. "Interesting. How so?"

"You've always been country." His country roots were something Valerie had always admired. Evan was hard-working, down to earth, and family-oriented. That hadn't seemed to waver over the years. "But when you took me to your store, that's when I understood your appreciation for history." Her fingers stilled. "You restored that barn and gave it new life. A new place in the community. You saved that building so its story can be told for generations to come. And that's beautiful, in my opinion."

He folded one of the empty paper bags, pondering her words. "Thank you. My store was definitely a labor of love. I really enjoyed fixing up that old dairy barn."

He grinned, and Valerie considered his answer. If the store was a labor of love, why hadn't he put the same care into his house? Evan had bought his home before Issy was born, but he'd left it as is, until now.

"Why haven't you done the same to your house?" she asked. It was something she'd pondered ever since she visited his store, but when Evan continued folding the bag instead of responding, the energy in the room shifted. She'd treaded too deeply for their current relationship—which was business only—and was just about to turn the conversation back to frozen vegetables when he responded.

"I wasn't ready to." The light in his eyes dimmed, and Valerie caught the reflection in his words. It only spiked her curiosity. What wasn't he ready for? The expense, the change, or something else?

The teapot whistled, and Evan went to the stove, changing the subject. "What kind of tea would you like?" He removed the pot from the burner, quieting the whistle but not the questions in her head. "There's chamomile, orange spice, lemon ginger, cinnamon vanilla," he continued, filling a mug with steaming water. "Mint and chai, too."

Valerie realized Evan wasn't going to elaborate on his answer, so she bit her nosy tongue. "Mint, please."

He dropped a tea bag into the mug and carried it to her, placing the steaming cup on the coffee table. "I would've guessed orange spice."

She gave him a soft smile. "My tastes have changed since we were together. I'm not really an orange spice kind of girl anymore."

He nodded. "There are probably quite a few things we don't know about each other, huh?"

"I'd guess so." She slid the mug toward her, across the coffee table. They'd been half their current age when they were together. "I'm sorry if I was prying with my question about your house. It's none of my business and you don't owe me an answer."

He looked pensive, as if he were considering her apology. Then he surprised her with, "My ex-wife and I bought the house a few months before Issy was born. It was a busy time."

His intense tone caught her attention. She nodded, giving Evan the chance to say whatever else he felt comfortable revealing.

He slid his fingers into the pocket of his jeans. "Once Issy arrived, we were so busy taking care of her and tackling life that the house wasn't our priority."

She cradled the mug with both hands. "That's understandable." She hadn't had babies of her own, but she could only imagine the amount of effort, time, and mental strength it took to raise a child.

"Years went by so quickly. Issy went from baby to toddler in the blink of an eye. Pretty soon she was a little girl, headed off to school with pigtails and a pink unicorn backpack."

Valerie smiled at the sweet visual.

"And sometime in those years my marriage fell apart," he added.

If Valerie hadn't been holding the tea with both hands, she would've dropped it to her lap.

Evan gave a slight shrug and continued, "I was trying to save our marriage instead of working on the house."

"I'm sorry," she offered, knowing the words were inadequate. She'd been told them countless times after her own divorce, though she wasn't sorry about the divorce itself. It was always an awkward sentiment to respond to. "I understand how tough that can be."

He nodded slowly. "Then I was a single dad and Issy always took priority. The house just hasn't been at the top of my to-do list, I guess."

Valerie pulled a knee toward her chest, sympathy seeping through her. "I get that."

He tilted his head, looking at the sunset for a beat before removing his hand from his pocket. "Enjoy your tea and there are more bags of frozen peas in the freezer if you need them."

"Thank you for making it for me." Valerie's fingers brushed the warm mug as she spoke. "See you in the morning?"

"I'll see you in the morning."

"Good night."

"Good night, Val."

As Evan retreated across the room, Valerie couldn't help but replay their conversation in her head. He'd shared a piece of his past with her, and she realized how little she knew about him. Maybe they had more in common than she thought. His use of her nickname had also grabbed her attention. The way he effortlessly shortened her name reminded her of an unspoken connection and sent flutters through her stomach. She hadn't realized how much she missed the simplicity of her nickname until now. The way Evan said it, with a touch of familiarity and tenderness, stirred something deep in her soul.

Taking a sip of her tea, Valerie's mind buzzed, and she wondered if she'd ever be able to fall asleep now.

Chapter Eight

Evan tossed the last remnants of the old carpet into the dumpster, relishing the sweat that clung to his body. Sweltering afternoon sun beat against his shoulders and back, but hard work calmed Evan. It was cathartic, and as he wiped his hands on his jeans, he was content. He'd put in plenty of hard work today.

Carpet and tile removed. Drop ceiling gone. Kitchen gutted.

But as he walked back toward his house, thoughts of flooring and sweat fizzled away, and his mind wound back to Val. How could it not? She was perched on his front porch steps, sitting next to his daughter. Issy cradled Val's computer on her lap, and they were both staring intently at the screen. Val pointed and said something that made Issy's eyes go wide. His daughter looked hypnotized.

Evan grinned.

"Dad, you've got to see this," Issy said as he neared. "We literally just built a house from scratch."

"Let me see." He joined them on the steps, sitting next to Issy.

Issy turned the laptop so he could see the screen. "Val showed me how to use her 3D rendering software and we designed the layout of this house. Now we're adding furniture and paint colors."

"Very cool." He enjoyed Issy's excitement most of all.

Val tipped forward, resting her elbow on her knee. She peeked around his daughter. "Issy's a fast learner." Her smile went from Evan to Issy. "You're picking this up faster than most adults."

"It's so fun." Issy clicked the keyboard a few times, changing the wall colors from beige to blue and then to pink. "Instant gratification. I'd play with this all day, if I could."

Evan glanced at his watch, knowing Issy was volunteering at Lilah's animal rescue tonight. "Hey, it's almost four."

Issy clicked one more time, turning the fictitious walls to a pale shade of green. "I better get going. Lilah took in a new pony yesterday, and he needs lots of loves." She slid the laptop toward Val. "Thanks so much for showing me all of this."

"Happy to." Val pulled the computer onto her lap. "Feel free to play around with the program. You can have my computer tomorrow while we're working on your house, and I'm happy to answer questions."

"Thank you." Issy glanced at Evan like she'd won the lottery. Then she bounced up from the stairs. "I'll be back at Grandma and Grandpa's late tonight. Like eight or nine?"

"What about dinner?" Evan asked.

"Lilah's feeding me. She said Trace is grilling hamburgers. I told Grandma already." Issy whistled for Skippy, who was aimlessly rolling around in the grass, paws in the air. He immediately popped up and ran to her side.

"All right. I'll see you later. Tell Lilah, Trace, and the kids hi from me."

Issy scratched Skippy's ears and gave a little wave. "Will do." She walked to her car with the pup gallivanting beside her.

Evan shifted his gaze to Val. "Thanks for taking the time to do that."

"My pleasure." She smiled and closed her laptop, setting it on the porch behind her. "She's a great kid."

His heart swelled. Issy was his pride and joy. There was no bigger compliment in his eyes. "How's your workplace injury?" he teased, redirecting the conversation.

Val raised her booted foot. "My ankle is feeling better, thanks to the peas."

"Glad they helped."

"And the tea."

He leaned forward, resting his forearms on his knees. "Got to make sure you're comfortable during your stay at The Carriage House. Hopefully, you'll leave an excellent review on Yelp."

"The service is impeccable. Five stars, for sure."

They shared a grin before Evan moved his gaze to the horse pastures, trying not to let their light banter yank his mind back to last night. He'd thought about it too much already.

When he'd offered to deliver groceries to The Carriage House, Evan had known he might run into Val. Deep down, he'd hoped for it. But he hadn't imagined discovering Val in her pajamas, sunset hues clinging to golden skin and long, curvy legs. The sight had stilled him. Frozen his boots straight to the floor. And he would have stayed there forever, taking her in, but self-preservation wouldn't allow it. His racing pulse was a clear sign he needed to focus on unloading groceries and keeping his stare decent—which was like holding the hot end of a branding iron.

Impossible.

"This humidity," Val uttered, breaking his train of thought. "I could cut the air with a knife."

"It's almost a hundred percent humidity today. Makes it feel a lot hotter than it is."

"Phew." She fanned both hands at her face. "It's completely different from the L.A. heat."

"Definitely different," he said, reminded that Val would leave Maple Bay in a few days. Her home was in California and Evan knew the barrier of distance. It wasn't something he wanted to re-enact. "Does Sal need any more help with cleanup?" He looked over his shoulder and through the front window. The camera crew had left. Only Sal and a few of his guys were still inside.

"I don't think so," she replied, just as her phone chimed. And buzzed. And chimed again. Val picked it up from the steps and tapped the screen. Her face fell.

"Everything okay?" Evan asked, but her eyes didn't leave the phone. She swiped and tapped until her mouth creaked open like a trapdoor. She inched close to her phone, reading intensely.

"How does he do that?"

"Who?" Evan wasn't sure she intended her question for him, but something was definitely wrong. Reluctantly, he bit his tongue as she scrolled.

When she finally set the phone down next to her, Val sighed, reminding him of a balloon losing the last of its air. "My ex-husband. Ryker."

"Oh." Her ex-husband had just texted her? Said something that upset her? Maybe their relationship wasn't really over. "Do you need some privacy? I can go back in the house if you need to call him."

Val shot Evan a look of disbelief, as if he'd just tried to shove her off the steps.

"Call him?" A breathy laugh escaped her. She shook her head. "I don't need to call him. We don't talk."

Confused, Evan scratched his head. However, growing up with sisters and having a teenage daughter had taught him to watch his mouth. Sometimes silence was the best answer in a touchy conversation. And this one felt dicey.

A long moment ticked by before Val sighed again. She set her elbows on her knees. "Sorry, I didn't mean to snap at you. I was just irritated. Not at you, though."

"I live with a teenager. My skin is thick. *That* wasn't snapping." The corner of her mouth curled slightly.

"Do you want to talk about it?" He wasn't sure he wanted to hear about her ex, but Val was obviously upset. If she needed a sympathetic ear, he'd listen.

Val flicked her gaze toward the pasture at the mares and babies lazing under tall oak trees. A buckskin colt ambled on lanky legs to his mom. As he nosed under the mare's flank and settled in to nurse, Val spoke.

"News of Ryker's new show is all over the internet."

"That's not good?" He kept his question gentle since Val and her ex weren't on speaking terms.

"I mean—" Val worried her bottom lip, thinking. "I wish him the best. It's not like I don't want him to be successful. I don't wish him ill-will."

"Divorce is hard." Evan knew the struggles that came with a broken marriage. He'd told Val a bit about his own divorce last night. His loose lips had surprised him since he didn't open up about that subject often.

Val looked at him, her eyes softening. "It is." Her nail found the seam of her jeans and she plucked it like a guitar string. "Don't get me wrong. There was a time when I wished he'd walk straight off a cliff, but I've worked past that. Mostly with therapy. But also through margaritas with Nina."

"Therapy and margaritas can work wonders."

"They can." She huffed a laugh. "Ryker and I weren't meant to be. It took me seven years to figure that out, but we're better off apart. Both of us."

Evan shifted on the wooden stairs, wondering what broke them. At the same time, he knew there were many issues that led to his own divorce. In his case, it hadn't mattered how hard he'd tried.

The damage to his marriage had spread like a crack in a windshield. There was no fixing it.

"It's not actually Ryker that irritated me. It's that I continue to take the brunt of the blame in the media," Val explained, and Evan hung on her words. "I keep getting blamed for our divorce and the end of LA Renovations. I hoped that storyline had been beaten to death and I wouldn't have to deal with it anymore, but the articles I just skimmed are rehashing the same false narrative about our divorce and the show, making me sound like the devil incarnate. Can't they just focus on him and leave me out of it?"

Evan cringed, not wanting to know what it was like to have your dirty laundry aired out for the world to see. He couldn't imagine how it would hurt to have the details of his divorce told through pictures and play-by-play articles. The divorce was hurt enough.

"Why do you read them?" he asked tentatively.

She turned to him, eyebrows pinched. "The articles?"

"Yeah." He placed a hand on the edge of the step, next to his thigh. "It seems painful. Like pouring salt in a wound."

"It is." Her quick answer took him by surprise, almost making him laugh. "But how I'm perceived in the public eye affects my career." She paused, worrying her lip again. "And now that one photo has resurfaced. I swear it's going to haunt me for the rest of my life."

"The spaghetti picture?" He winced for her, picturing the photo of her and Ryker that surfaced just before their show had been cancelled.

Wrapping her hands around her elbows in a self-hug, she nodded. "That's the one."

Evan had seen the photo, but not in the tabloids or online. He heard about it from his mom and Issy. In fact, he'd endured an entire dinner conversation about how sad they were to see their favorite TV couple break up and the show end. Evan had nearly choked on his mashed potatoes when Issy brought the photo up on her phone, showing him a tense scene in a fancy restaurant. Val had been red-faced, her mouth wide open. She was yelling and pointing at Ryker—who had red-sauce pasta slopped down the front of his white shirt. Gawkers surrounded them. The server had his hand over his mouth.

"That photo makes me look like a crazy person," Val said, and Evan couldn't disagree. "It also got my show cancelled."

"It was cancelled because of that photo?"

She gave a shrug. "Viewership was down, and the network knew Ryker and I were planning to separate. They said there was nowhere to go with the storyline if we divorced. So, for the last season of the show, Ryker and I were acting, trying to be the happy couple that we definitely were not."

"Wow." Evan had not expected that answer. "That must've been horrible."

She nodded. "I was trying to hold on to two pieces of my life that were spiraling out of control, and it turned into a tornado. That photo was the last straw. It cemented the network's decision to cancel the show. It was also one of my lowest moments. I'm not proud of it, but it also doesn't tell the entire story of what got me to that point."

In that moment, Val looked small. Like her body had physically shrunk under the weight of what she'd told him. He didn't know exactly what was squashing her—the recollection of her divorce or the worry of what would come because of the resurfaced photo. But in her silence, Evan realized he'd judged her just like everyone else had. He'd made his own conclusions based on a single photo the media had harped on, not knowing what Val had been through in the past two decades. He was familiar with what her life looked like on TV, but sitting with her on his front step, he wanted to know what her life had been like behind the camera.

Val cleared her throat and gave him a stiff smile. "I'm sorry. I didn't mean to unload on you. It's not your problem."

He wanted to tell her he didn't mind. That he appreciated her honesty and could sympathize with her more than she knew. But he also didn't want to upset her further. Instead, he asked, "Do you want to go get some ice cream?"

Chapter Nine

Valerie and Evan sat side by side in the UTV, hurtling down a country road much faster than she would've guessed. Wind and dust whipped and tangled her hair. On both sides of the road, stalky cornfields stretched out in every direction, mixing to a green blur, and Valerie found solace in the impromptu road trip. The howling wind and rumbling motor made it impossible to have a conversation, and the lack of talk gave her space to collect her thoughts.

She hadn't meant to tell Evan about Ryker or the photo. It had just spilled out, spurred by the way he'd looked at her on his front porch steps—with empathy instead of judgement. His presence had blanketed her and eased the words right out of her mouth, which was a feat because she was rarely vulnerable. She'd rather talk about subjects that couldn't hurt her—like architecture and design.

Pushing hair back from her face, she glanced over at Evan.

"We're almost there," he shouted. His voice competed with the rumbling engine, sounding worried that she'd had enough of the ride.

She offered him a smile and looked back at the cornfields. For a moment, she closed her eyes and leaned back, enjoying the warm wind and the sweet smell of crops and earth. The strength of Evan's arm brushed against her shoulder, moving with the sway of the UTV, and provided a sense of comfort she couldn't quite explain.

Each sensation calmed her, better than any yoga or meditation class she'd taken. They forced away thoughts of how her reputation and career had been destroyed by the media and fears of it happening again, just when things were looking up for her. The present moment allowed her to ignore the past and the future. She was simply enjoying the freedom of a country road.

As the UTV slowed, Valerie opened her eyes and lifted her head from the headrest.

"Sorry, I should've warned you how dusty that ride would be." Evan drove through the gravel lot and parked on the side of the feed store. "You've got a pretty good dirt-tan going on now."

Valerie looked at Evan. "Did you say *dirt-tan*?" But as she asked, she understood what he was referring to. Evan was smiling and his teeth looked extra white against the dust that masked his face. The crinkles at the edges of his eyes were penciled with filth.

A laugh escaped her. "Oh, my—" She touched her cheek and felt grit. "We're a mess."

Evan turned off the engine. He set one arm on top of the steering wheel and smirked. "I'm a mess, but you make dirt look good."

Valerie's stomach fluttered. Her cheeks warmed, and it wasn't because of the sticky humidity. Pressing her lips together, she hoped her dirt-tan covered her blush. "I'm ready for ice cream."

Evan winked and got out of the UTV. "Come on. Let's get some."

They headed into the store through a tall, open barn door where a few employees were loading feed bags onto a truck bed. Valerie expected comments about their dirty state, but they were only greeted with waves and friendly hellos as they wandered through the store. When they neared the adorable parlor, Evan stepped behind the glass countertop filled with tubs of ice cream. He washed his hands in the sink.

"You need help, Evan?" a woman called from the dressing room area, where she was helping a customer.

"I got it, Gloria. Thanks." Evan continued scrubbing his hands with soap. As he did, Valerie peered through the glass counter, scanning the array of colors and flavors.

"There's so many yummy options." She read the signs next to each tub of ice cream. "Cookies and Cream. Caramel Apple. Cake Batter. How am I supposed to decide?" She was nearly drooling.

"Let me know if there's something you want to try." He dried his hands with a red-checkered dish towel. "Or I can make you a big bowl with a bunch of different flavors."

Valerie grinned at the suggestion of a mounded bowl boasting every color of the rainbow. It was tempting, especially because she rarely had ice cream anymore. Being on camera, she was always watching her weight. It was exhausting, and today she didn't have the energy to deal with counting calories. Looking up at Evan, she asked, "What's your favorite flavor?"

She'd intended to narrow her choices, but something about her question stilled Evan. He set the dish towel down, the sparkle in his blue eyes wavering for a moment—longer than necessary during a conversation about ice cream.

He picked up a metal scoop and opened the glass cabinet. "Cookie Dough is the most popular. Issy loves the German Chocolate Fudge. But my favorite is the Candy Concoction." Evan leaned into the case and pulled the curved scoop through a tub in the center. He rolled the cream until it was the size of a tennis ball. "It's vanilla ice cream mixed with chopped Peppermint Patties, M&M's, and—"

Valerie's gaze jerked up. "Candy Canes?"

In reply, Evan met her gaze with a tender smile. He grabbed a sugar cone and pressed the scoop of Candy Concoction on the top. He handed it to her over the counter. "Do you want to try it?"

Silently, Valerie reached out. She slid her fingers around the textured cone, grazing Evan's hand as she did. Tingles wound up her arm and settled in her chest, though she wasn't sure what caused them. Was it Evan's touch? Or that he was handing her a memory from years past? A memory that had meant a lot to her.

"You found a company that makes ice cream just like we used to?" She gripped the cone tightly.

"Mm-hmm," he confirmed before reaching back into the glass case and digging into the same tub. As he scooped, Valerie remembered the first time they'd made the treat together, back in college.

It was winter break, when Evan had driven eight long hours from Maple Bay to her shoebox-sized apartment in Lincoln, Nebraska. Valerie hadn't gone home for Christmas that year, because for her, home was a vague concept. She and her sister had been raised by their mother, who had a string of boyfriends that went in and out of their lives. Their mom had a new boyfriend that Christmas. Valerie hadn't met him yet, but her mother was infatuated with him, just like all the other men she had dated. So when Valerie discovered her mom would be celebrating Christmas with her new boyfriend's family, Valerie decided not to make the drive "home" to northern Kansas. Especially since her sister wouldn't be there, not able to afford a flight from where she was attending college in Chicago.

When Evan found this out, he insisted Valerie shouldn't be alone for the holidays. She'd said she was fine and would pick up extra shifts at the restaurant, but deep down she was hurt by her mother's choices. And lonely. So when Evan arrived at her door Christmas day after braving hundreds of miles of icy roads, she'd fought tears and hugged him like Santa himself had arrived on her doorstep. They'd only been dating for a few months, yet he'd gone above and beyond for her.

That evening, after a celebratory dinner of grilled cheese and tomato soup, they'd craved dessert, but the only store open was the gas station down the block. Together, they'd picked out a pint of vanilla ice cream, a peppermint patty in the shape of an evergreen tree, a bag of red and green M&M's, and two candy canes. When they got back to her apartment, they chopped and crushed the candy and mixed everything together. Valerie still remembered how sweet the bowl of ice cream had been, as she'd cuddled with Evan on her couch, enjoying their Christmas treat and watching *It's a Wonderful Life*. Decades later, she'd never forgotten that feeling—that someone cared so much about her that he'd dropped everything just to put a smile on her face.

"I can't believe you found a company that makes this exact flavor." She stared at Evan, dumbfounded, as he plopped another big scoop on a cone.

He closed the glass case. "It's a local creamery. They make a few special flavors for the store. I asked them to make this one. It's always been my favorite."

Valerie's heart stilled, not sure how to respond. Had the memory surrounding the ice cream meant as much to him as to her?

"It's your favorite?" she asked. A shard of gooey candy cane dropped to her thumb. "Still?"

"I've never found anything I like better." The certainty in his stare forced her thoughts to pinball, bouncing from the past to the present. In all honesty, she'd never tasted anything so sweet, but it had nothing to do with the ingredients.

Just then, a man and little boy appeared next to Valerie. Evan's gaze went to them.

"Hey, guys." He set the cone he'd made for himself in a metal holder. "You here for your post-baseball ice cream cones?"

The little boy waved a leather mitt in the air and told Evan about the pop ball he'd caught. As his dad proudly told the rest of the story, Valerie smiled and stepped to the side. She took a seat on one of the rotating metal stools and licked her ice cream cone. The rich vanilla swirled with the crunch of chocolate and peppermint, and Valerie paused, savoring the sweetness. It melted into her, making her chest clench. Was she so jaded that she'd forgotten how good she and Evan had been at one time? Had she pushed away wonderful memories, only to remember hard times?

She licked her lips. *Maybe.*

Putting two spoons in a bowl full of chocolate ice cream, Evan said, "Enjoy," and handed the bowl to the man. "And good job on the pop fly today. Keep it up, buddy."

The little boy ran in place and said "thank you" between a few squeaks. As he and his dad walked off, Evan retrieved his cone from the metal stand and turned back to Valerie.

"So, I have to know—" he started, forcing Valerie to pause mid-bite, worried what he might ask. "What does your house look like?"

The tension in her chest eased, thankful he hadn't circled back to their shared past. She wasn't quite ready for the depth of that conversation. Not today. "My house?"

"Yeah. Tell me about your house, back in L.A." Evan licked the bottom edge of his ice cream, catching the drips. "You're getting to see every nook and cranny of my place. I think it's fair you tell me about yours."

She grinned. This was a topic she could handle. "What do you want to know?"

Evan squinted, looking thoughtful. "Where's it located? In the city? By the ocean?"

She dabbed her mouth with a napkin. "A little of both. I have a condo on the beach, in Santa Monica."

"Is that close to L.A.?"

"Technically? Yes," she replied. "It's about fifteen miles from my condo to downtown, mostly highway. But if you get on I-10 at the wrong time of day, it can easily take two hours."

"Two hours to drive fifteen miles?" Evan looked disgusted. "That's crazy."

She shrugged. "You have to pick your drive times wisely." Back when she and Ryker were married, they had an obnoxiously large condo downtown, only a few miles from HomeTV's offices. After the divorce, Valerie needed a change of scenery. She'd picked a one-bedroom condo with an ocean view, loving the outdoor space where she could sit and listen to the waves. She was within walking distance of restaurants and shops at the pier, but she'd mostly kept to herself, soaking in the solitude. "I avoid rush hour, at all costs."

"I would too." Evan took a big bite of ice cream. After swallowing, he added, "The biggest traffic jam around here involves slow moving tractors, or a loose cow."

She grinned. "It's a little more laid back around here." During her brief stay in Maple Bay, the town had already had a calming effect on her, almost like sitting on her deck, listening to the waves.

"I like moving slow," he replied, causing Valerie to reflect on the constant whirlwind that consumed her life. She was always on the go, constantly striving towards goals and projects.

After her divorce and losing LA Renovations, she'd struggled to find a new rhythm, attempting to fill every minute of her day with activity. She'd thrown herself into multiple house flips, purging her time and money on projects where she could make a difference and turn a profit. Any spare moment was spent researching her next potential flip. It was easier that way—when she didn't have to think about what had hurt her.

"Moving slow can be nice sometimes," she admitted, considering the pockets of unexpected downtime she'd had in the past few days. There'd been many simple pleasures that had filled them. A steaming bubble bath. Witnessing breathtaking sunsets over the lake. Getting a dirt-tan.

The edges of her lips turned up in a smile.

"I'd argue that it's nice all the time." Evan plucked two napkins from the back counter and handed one to her. "What's your color scheme in your condo?"

She took the napkin, remembering their conversation about Evan's color scheme and wallpaper choices . . . right before she hammered into the wall and fell into his arms. Her cheeks warmed again. "White," she replied, before swallowing.

"White?" Evan cocked his head, looking perplexed. "I know I'm not a designer, but that sounds like one color. Not an entire scheme."

"Many different shades of white," she defended her design choice. "It's a monochromatic scheme."

"Hmm." His response was barely more than a mumble. "Interesting."

"I have pops of color throughout," she clarified, though she wasn't sure why. She'd put a lot of thought into decorating her condo. "It's a clean look. Simple and consistent." She'd surrounded herself with white to create stability and simplicity, something she'd desperately needed.

"Sounds nice," he concluded. Then he greeted another customer, leaving Valerie to psychoanalyze her design choices. Would she make the same choices now? As Valerie mulled this over, Evan continued taking ice cream orders. In between helping customers, he peppered Valerie with questions. *Do you have any pets?* No, but she enjoyed cat-sitting for her neighbor, a sassy woman in her seventies who often vacationed with her girlfriends. *How long did you work for HomeTV?* Seven years—the same amount of time she'd been married, though she left out the last part. *What's your favorite part about renovating?* The final reveal to the homeowner. Seeing the happiness spurred by just the right combination of design.

Valerie wanted to know more about Evan as well, but he hadn't given her a chance, continuing with question after question between scooping ice cream. However, she gathered a few tidbits from his friendly chats with customers and considered her findings during their drive back to the inn. As the tranquil countryside passed by, she considered what Evan's daily life looked like. She'd learned that he coached youth football and helped the high school kids with weekly rodeo practices. He rode every other Sunday during Cowboy Church and was heavily involved with the local rodeo every summer. He did all that on top of running a feed store, managing his family's stable, and being a single dad? Maybe his life wasn't as slow-paced as he made it out to be.

When they parked in front of The Carriage House, Valerie said, "Thanks so much for the ice cream. I really enjoyed that." She wanted to ask him to join her for a glass of wine or a cup of tea, but knew his parents were waiting on him for dinner, so instead she stepped out of the UTV.

Circling the front of the vehicle, Evan joined her near the inn's front door. "I'm glad. I enjoyed it too." He slid a thumb into his pocket, looking like he had more to say. Her heartbeat grew faster, and just as she found the nerve to ask him to join her for a drink, Evan turned toward the inn. "Let me get that for you." He stepped toward the door, his chivalrous gesture quieting her invitation. But the door popped open before he got to it.

Hazel poked her head out. "Hey! I thought I heard an engine." She smiled and swung the door fully open. She was holding a broom. Her red curls were piled on top of her head in a messy bun. "I was just finishing up in here. You guys coming to supper? Joyce just called and said it'll be ready in a half-hour."

Valerie was taken aback by her question. "Oh, I . . . no. I don't want to intrude." Not to mention she hadn't been invited.

"Intrude?" Hazel looked aghast. "We'd love to have you. Come on. Joyce is making pork chops and potato salad and she'd be happy as a clam to have you as a guest."

Valerie looked at Evan. He didn't look as surprised as she felt.

"Mom always makes enough food to feed an army," he said. "And she'd love to have you over. Actually, she'd probably be mad at me if I didn't bring you."

Hazel nodded vigorously. "She sure would."

"I'm dirty." Valerie held her arms out, displaying the evidence.

"You've got time to wash up." Hazel waved off Valerie's second excuse. "I've got a few things to finish in the Carriage House. You can clean up and then walk over with me."

"You should come," Evan said, seriously.

Valerie's racing thoughts stilled for a beat. A minute ago, she hadn't had the nerve to ask Evan to extend their conversation. Now she was being invited to join him and his family for supper? Twenty years ago, that was the invitation she would have killed for.

"Okay," she agreed, still feeling like she was intruding.

"Yay!" Hazel squealed and reached for Valerie, giving her a gentle but excited tug toward the door. "We'll meet you over there, Evan." She waved him off with her broom. "Looks like you need to clean up, too. What exactly were you guys doing?"

Valerie followed Hazel into the inn. "Getting ice cream," she replied, but as the UTV rumbled off, Valerie wondered if they'd done so much more than that. Or was she imagining the sparks that had flown between her and Evan?

Chapter Ten

When Hazel and Val arrived, Evan was setting a stack of plates on the kitchen island. At first sight of Val, his grip slipped, and he put the dishes down harder than he'd intended. As they clattered against the countertop, Val's gaze shot to him. She gave him a warm, timid smile.

His heart bounced. *God, she was gorgeous.*

Standing in the doorway, Val's fresh face and olive skin glowed. Her dark, damp hair was woven into a braid that fell over her shoulder and across her chest. And her green eyes had changed. Her gaze had warmed up and softened, and that was the most beautiful thing of all.

"We're here," Hazel announced, balancing a latticed pie on one arm and presenting Val with the other.

Evan's mom stepped away from the crockpot of baked beans she'd been stirring. She set down the spoon. "Oh, we're so glad you came!" Wiping her hands on her apron, she walked straight to Val and gave her a big hug.

"Thank you for having me," Val replied, hugging back.

"Happy to," Joyce said. "Come on in. Make yourself comfortable. I hope you're hungry. Can I get you something to drink? Evan, get her something to drink. Introduce her to the family while I finish up the beans. Everyone's outside in the backyard."

His mom turned back toward the crockpot, her slew of statements making Evan grin. "Can I get you an iced tea? Water? Pop? Wine? Beer?"

"An iced tea would be great," Val replied, looking like she wasn't sure what to do with herself.

"You want one too, Hazel?" he asked.

"Yes, please." Hazel placed the pie on the counter.

"Is there anything I can help with?" Val asked, while Evan retrieved two glasses from a cabinet. "I feel horrible not bringing anything."

"Nonsense," Joyce said. "You just relax and enjoy. You're our guest."

"Okay, thank you." Val stepped around the island toward Evan, still looking like a fish out of water. "I thought this was just a casual weeknight dinner." Her eyes were wide.

Confused, Evan looked around. Food covered the island. An enormous bowl of his mom's famous blue cheese potato salad sat next to a platter of meat, cheese, and crackers. There was a fruit salad and green bean casserole, not to mention the crockpot of maple beans and the pork chops baking in the oven. He shrugged. "It is."

"*This* is a casual weeknight dinner?"

"For the Westons?" He raised a pitcher of iced tea. "Yes." His mom loved to cook for her family. Dinners like this happened at least twice a week. "Actually, only half the family is here tonight. You should see what this kitchen cranks out for Sunday supper when everyone is here and cooking."

Val's mouth went slack.

"You should come on Sunday," Joyce said over her shoulder, plopping a dollop of honey in the beans. "Bring the entire crew." The excitement in his mom's voice was palatable.

"She loves to feed people," he whispered to Val. "You can't say no."

Val grinned and shifted her attention to his mom. "That's very generous of you. I'm sure the crew would love that, but only if you let us contribute. I make a mean artichoke-spinach dip. Nina does these amazing spicy beef empanadas, and Sal can pick out a bottle of wine like no other."

His mom smiled, the corners of her eyes crinkling. "Deal."

"Great." Val sighed, looking more relaxed now that his mom had given her approval to contribute.

Adding lemon slices to the iced teas, Evan handed a glass to Val, acknowledging the warmth that had spread through his chest while Val, Hazel, and his mom chatted. "Here you go."

"Thank you." She took a long sip, her dark eyelashes lowering and skimming her cheeks. When Evan's gaze got stuck on her pink lips, he turned and delivered the other tea to Hazel. He couldn't daydream about kissing Val. He'd fought through the tempting thoughts earlier, as they'd shared ice cream and conversation. The pull to take her in his arms had only increased when they'd been standing in front of The Carriage House. It was a good thing Hazel had intervened, or Evan might've kissed the dirt right off Val's mouth.

"Let's go outside." He pushed aside his ridiculous fantasies. "I'll introduce you to everyone."

Evan led Val past the kitchen table and out the sliding glass door. On the deck, Jesse waved from the patio table.

"Hey," Jesse said with a smile. He was leaning forward, entertaining baby G in his bouncy chair. Jesse's border collie, Blue, lay obediently at the base of the chair. "How's it going?"

"Good." Evan shut the sliding door behind Val. "Just wanted to introduce Val to everyone. I know you guys already met, but—" Evan faltered, wanting to rephrase his choice of words. Val and Jesse had met at the inn when she'd first arrived. He wasn't referring to many years ago, or the secret the three of them were keeping. "She hasn't met your kids. Or Kat and Creed," he clarified.

Jesse cocked an eyebrow, but Val stepped forward, not missing a beat. "Is this your handsome boy?" She bent down to get a good look at the baby.

A wide smile took over Jesse's face and Evan's clumsy words were forgotten. "It sure is. This is Gene." He bounced the baby's chair, and Gene kicked his legs in excitement. "He's named after my dad, and we've been calling him Baby G. Though that nickname probably won't stick once he's in high school."

Val chuckled. "How sweet." In response, Baby G gave a happy murmur and showed off his chubby cheeks.

"Thank you. He's a happy boy." Jesse kept his beaming gaze on his son, and a rush of pride hit Evan. His little brother was such a good father. Jesse had been in a state of bliss since he and Hazel brought Baby G into this world just a few months ago. But he'd already proven his worth as a father, two times over. In addition to Baby G, Jesse had two daughters. After their sister Sarah's tragic passing six years ago, Jesse had adopted their niece Charlie. At the time, Charlie had been a baby, not much older than Baby G was now. But Jesse gave up his rambling single life and jumped into fatherhood with both boots. Then, when Hazel came along and stole his heart, he'd gained a stepdaughter as well—Grace. Now they were a family and Evan had never seen his brother happier.

"He's going to be quite the cowboy. I just know it." Evan grinned at his bouncing, kicking nephew. "It won't be long until he puts those active little legs in a saddle and keeps up with his sisters." Jesse laughed, and Evan looked up. "Speaking of, here come Charlie and Grace."

The girls had been riding near the barn but started toward them when he and Val had stepped onto the deck. Now, Charlie and Grace were trotting their horses toward the house. Behind them, Evan's dad walked alongside their sister Kat and her husband Creed.

"Uncle Evan!" Charlie waved enthusiastically from the back of her palomino pony. Her blonde pigtails bounced. Grace gave them a sweet smile.

"Who's your friend?" Charlie asked, never one to be shy.

Evan introduced Val to the girls and then to Kat and Creed.

"It's nice to finally meet you," Kat said, coming up the stairs and onto the deck. Her Jack Russell, Thelma, bound up behind her. Kat's older terrier, Louise, was cradled in their dad's arms—her favorite spot to nap. "I've been hearing all about you for the past few days. Are you whipping my brother's house into shape?"

"It's coming along really nicely," Val replied. "We finished the floors downstairs, and the crew was tiling the upstairs bathroom this afternoon."

As the conversation continued, Val got more comfortable, which set Evan at ease. He temporarily forgot the unspoken past that hung between them. Charlie's antics helped. She told Val all about her pony and showed her a few tricks—like how the pony could nod her head on cue. Charlie would've continued entertaining everyone for the next hour, but Hazel told the girls to unsaddle their horses and wash up for supper.

Inside the house, Val helped Kat set the table and Evan caught himself eavesdropping as he made a pitcher of lemonade. The women had found a shared interest—Chicago, where Kat had lived, before moving back to Maple Bay.

"I don't miss the hustle and bustle," Kat said, while setting plates on the table. "But there's so much to see and do. Plays, museums, concerts. Actually, Creed and I spent a weekend there a few months ago. Got to see some friends and a Luke Bryant concert. Right, honey?"

"Sure did," Creed answered from the kitchen. He was taking the pork chops out of the oven. "Kat got this cowboy to brave the big city." He winked at his wife, and they shared a smile.

"How long has your sister lived there?" Kat asked Val.

"Since college." Val situated silverware next to a plate. "I love visiting. There're so many beautiful buildings downtown. Lots of historic architecture."

As Val described a few of her favorite buildings, passion bled into her words, and it was hard to concentrate on anything else. Evan had nearly added salt to the lemonade instead of sugar but caught himself at the last second.

When they sat down for dinner, Evan took the seat between Val and his mom, noticing how his mom had moved over one chair from her usual spot. He guessed she was intentionally seating him next to Val, but he didn't mind. Now he wouldn't have to strain to hear Val's sweet voice.

"Evan, would you say grace?" his mom asked. "You don't mind, do you, Valerie?"

"Oh, of course not." Val straightened against the back of her chair. "That'd be wonderful."

His mom set her hand on Evan's, cueing the family to lock hands around the table and bow their heads, which gave Evan and Val a single moment to themselves. He caught her gaze and offered his hand; the anticipation forcing his heart to skip. When she wrapped her delicate fingers around his, a ribbon of warmth spun through him. He'd never had to concentrate so hard on thanking God for His blessings.

"Amen," everyone said at the end of Evan's prayer. Val slipped her hand from his, and Evan immediately picked up his knife and fork, stunned by the heat that left him with her hand. The emptiness made him wish for the slide of her palm once again. Trying to fill the void with something, he put a forkful of potato salad in his mouth and focused on the bacon-and-blue-cheese goodness.

Throughout the meal, conversation flowed. Stories were shared. There was laughter and Evan couldn't get over how well Val fit in. Her presence was natural—like she'd been part of the family all along. Which made Evan wonder what could've been if they'd made it to the altar. Could they have made it work? *Should* they have made it work?

Carving off another piece of pork chop, Evan knew the answer to his own questions: No.

Maybe they could've worked it out—if he'd followed her to L.A., or if Val had been willing to attend a graduate school in Minneapolis. But if they'd stayed together, he wouldn't have Issy, and Evan wouldn't trade his daughter for anything. He wouldn't consider a reality that didn't include his Isabel.

"You got a husband, Valerie?" Charlie asked, like she'd stumbled on an extra present under the Christmas tree. Her eyes sparkled with curiosity and Evan stopped chewing, wondering where she was going with this question.

"A husband?" Val gave an uncomfortable laugh and a shake of her head. "No, I don't have one of those. Too busy with work." She smiled politely, digging a spoon into her baked beans.

Charlie tilted her head and scrunched her nose. "Why you too busy?"

Hazel set a hand on Charlie's shoulder. "Charlie, I don't think that's any of your business," she gently scolded her daughter. "Why don't you tell Val about—"

"Why not?" Charlie looked genuinely confused. "Grandma is always saying that Uncle Evan needs a wife, and I like Valerie. I'm just asking why she's too busy to be Uncle Evan's wife."

Evan sucked in a breath and got a green bean lodged at the back of his throat. Stunned, he let go of his fork. It rattled against the plate as he coughed. All attention turned to him.

"You okay?" Val asked, grabbing hold of his arm, her eyes wide.

His mom turned and whacked him on the back a few times. "Chew your food, Evan. Goodness. Do I need to give you the Heimlich?"

Covering his mouth, Evan hacked again, clearing his throat. "I'm okay." His voice was raspy, and he waved off his dad, who was now standing, looking ready to spring into action. "Just got a green bean down the wrong pipe." Grabbing his lemonade, he took a big swallow, giving himself a moment to recover.

"Good." His mom patted him on the back, now convinced he didn't need her help—with the green bean, at least. "Charlie, you know your uncle is sensitive about dating and marriage."

The lemonade just about spurt from Evan's mouth, especially when he caught his mom wink at Charlie. Wanting to get a few words in before this conversation went completely off the rails, Evan forced a swallow. But his mom continued quickly.

"Remember, he told us no more matchmaking after we tried to set him up with your teacher?"

Charlie pursed her lips. "But you and Mommy said—"

"Okay, new subject," Hazel interrupted, giving Evan an apologetic smile and an uncomfortable chuckle. "Who's ready for dessert?"

"Me!" Charlie's attention flipped to apple pie, but the same couldn't be said for the rest of his family. Jesse's mouth cracked open, resembling the can of worms Charlie had opened. Creed was on the verge of laughing, but had enough sense to hide it behind a cough. And every woman at the table was now pretending they hadn't been gossiping about his love life, or trying to meddle in it.

Val was quiet, and Evan wanted the conversation to go anywhere other than where it was at.

He cleared his throat and wiped his mouth with a napkin. "Apple pie sounds great."

Chapter Eleven

After dinner, Valerie walked back to the inn with Hazel, Jesse, and their kids. They said goodnight, and Valerie thanked them again for a wonderful evening, but when she got to her room, she wasn't ready to settle in. Questionable feelings had wiggled their way into her head, and she wasn't sure what to do with them. Instead of putting on her pajamas, Valerie grabbed a light sweater, threw it over her arm, and headed back outside.

As she walked toward the lake, she passed Jesse and Hazel's home—an adorable robin's-egg-blue cottage that overlooked the water. In the dark, it was hard not to peer through the front window and into the kitchen, where Jesse held Baby G like a football. With his other arm, he pulled Hazel to his chest. When he kissed the top of her head, Valerie's chest tightened and she looked away, feeling like she was intruding on an intimate moment. They were such a sweet couple, radiating love for each other and their kids. The entire Weston family seemed to have an immense amount of love for each other. That was clear to Valerie, even after a single dinner.

And she couldn't help but wonder what that would be like. To be part of a big, tight-knit family that enjoyed each other's company. Living close to your parents and siblings. To be a part of each other's daily lives, sharing meals and laughter.

The idea was foreign to Valerie, yet she yearned for it—but it wasn't her reality or her family. Here, she was a guest. An outsider looking in on the type of family she wished for: loving and supportive. A circle of people that were there for each other, through thick and thin. The Westons appeared to be built on a solid foundation—a concrete slab that even the strongest storm couldn't break. Valerie's family was more like a tent, always on the verge of blowing away. She and her sister had hammered the stakes back into the ground many times, trying to keep the entire structure from collapsing. It was a continuous process with their lovesick mother and absentee father.

As she strode down the dirt path that edged Maple Leaf Lake, Valerie tried to focus on anything other than Evan, but it was proving impossible. She couldn't get him out of her head, so she picked up her pace, moving into a speed walk and zoning in on objects as she passed them. *Tall oak trees. A small rowboat pulled ashore and tied to a rock. Croaking frogs and a hooting owl.* When she broke from a patch of trees, she was surprised by how much ground she'd covered. Suddenly realizing she was in Evan's backyard, she slowed her stride.

The house was dark, a few hundred feet from the lake, and Valerie doubted anyone was milling about at this hour. The crew was back at the inn or tucked into their respective RVs for the night. Evan and Issy were staying at Joyce and Gene's, so Valerie startled when she discovered a vehicle near the shoreline. It was a truck, parked with the bed facing the water.

She halted. Was that what she thought it was?

A memory urged her feet forward and became clearer with each step. The truck was a nineteen forty-nine Chevy. Rounded hubs gleamed in the moonlight, showing off the cherry-red paint. A pair of fuzzy, white dice hung from the rearview mirror.

"How had I *not* noticed this out here?" she asked herself, nearing the truck. She'd ridden in that cab many times . . . years ago.

Suddenly, a rustling noise startled her, and she caught movement out of the corner of her eye. She jumped and let out a yelp. Someone or something was in the truck's bed. She should've brought her pepper spray. What was she thinking, wandering off alone like this?

"Val?" Evan's voice carried through the night and cut through her racing thoughts. His form appeared as he sat up in the bed. Twisting toward her, the surprise on his face became highlighted by the moon. "What are you doing out here?"

She released a tight breath. "Goodness." She paused a second, allowing her heart to drop back into her chest. "You scared me."

"Same." He placed a hand on the edge of the bed. "I don't run into too many people out here at nine o'clock." He edged a line between sarcasm and curiosity.

She took another breath to settle her bouncing nerves. "Just going for an after-dinner walk."

"In the dark? By yourself?"

"Needed some wind-down time before bed." She'd wanted to clear her head of Evan and had somehow walked straight to him. Was the universe trying to get them back together?

He nodded, slowly. "Me too. I needed some fresh air."

Steadying herself, Valerie rested a hand on the truck door. The window was open, and her fingers curved over the smooth, rounded edge. Immediately, her mind shifted to a younger version of Evan, leaning out the window, his muscular arm hung on the door, and his smile capturing her whole heart.

She yanked her hand from the truck like she'd been shocked.

"You still have your truck." She looked at Evan for an answer, but she hadn't asked a question. The shiny red paint job was new and the bench seat reupholstered in tufted black leather, but the same dice hung from the rearview mirror. Usually, she couldn't identify much about a vehicle. She didn't care to. But this truck had been burned into her brain.

"I do." He scooted forward to sit on the tailgate. "I keep it in my parents' shed. Just take it out on special occasions."

"Today's a special occasion?"

"Nah. Just needed a little space. I think better out here. It's here, on a boat, or in a saddle. And I didn't think my horse would appreciate a ride this late."

She nodded, though she wasn't sure Evan could see her response in the dark.

"You can join me, if you'd like," he offered, glancing over his shoulder at her. "The tailgate has room for two."

She remembered. When Evan's gaze stayed steady, anxiety percolated in her chest. This was the opposite of what she'd intended to do—walk off the pull she felt to Evan—but maybe this was what she needed. No cameras. No audience. Just her and Evan.

Forcing her feet to move, Valerie walked to the back of the truck. Evan slid off the tailgate and stood, offering his hand. Tentatively, she took it, ignoring the zing of attraction that got stronger every time they touched. He guided her onto the tailgate and took a seat beside her. The truck shifted under his weight, and she threw the sweater she'd been carrying over her shoulders like a cape. She needed a layer between them.

"Kind of ironic that we're back here, isn't it?" she asked, looking out over the dark lake.

Evan tipped forward, curling his fingers over the edge of the tailgate. "Yep."

He'd driven this truck to visit her that memorable Christmas in college. They'd sat on the tailgate, sharing kisses and dreams the following summer. And they'd been slow dancing in the bed, the hum of music coming from the cab, when Evan had fallen to a knee and pulled a ring from his pocket. She'd been crazy about him, stupidly assuming love could transcend all of life's bumps. She'd said yes, even though their dreams were pulling them down separate paths.

Valerie scanned the pebbled shoreline and slow lap of water. "How come your family doesn't know about me?" The second she said it, she felt silly, like a schoolgirl wanting her crush to acknowledge her existence. She quickly added, "I just thought they'd know about us. My mom and sister heard plenty about you. If they ran into you today, they'd know who you were." She cringed and grabbed the collar of her cardigan with both hands, tugging it tightly across her neck.

"I told them about you." Evan angled his shoulders toward her, and Valerie stayed quiet, finding it awkward to grapple with feelings from nearly two decades ago. At one time, she'd been in love with this man. She'd been heartbroken when they separated, but Evan had moved on quickly. Within a few months after their broken engagement, he'd started dating someone new—who he married and started a family with.

Valerie shook her head, wanting to brush away her question. She was being sensitive because of the wonderful evening they'd shared, or maybe because she was sitting with him in the truck he'd proposed to her in. Regardless, neither of them would be the people they were today if they'd stayed together. "I'm sorry. Please forget I asked." She'd shared enough embarrassing information with him today when she opened up about Ryker. "Your family is lovely. You're very lucky. I really enjoyed having dinner with them." *And you.*

"Val," he started, before pausing for a few uncomfortable beats. "You and football were the only things I ever thought about, but I was twenty-two and had a lot to learn about life and love. I should've never asked you to give up your scholarship and your dreams to follow mine. That was very selfish of me and I'm truly sorry I did that."

She loosened the grip on her cardigan, eased by his genuine words. "I appreciate that, but you don't have to apologize. We were young," she admitted, with a glance at him. "We both had a lot to learn." If she'd given up her full ride scholarship and hadn't gotten her Master's at UCLA, she would've always wondered what she could've accomplished. If she'd married Evan and given up her own dreams, that question would've lingered in the back of her mind.

Putting his hands on his knees, Evan looked out over the lake like a lighthouse scanning for a boat. "But I need you to know that I told my family plenty about you while we were together. I just didn't get the chance to tell them about our engagement before we broke up. I wanted to tell them in person and with you."

Valerie released the neck of her sweater, letting her hands fall to her thighs. "Are you saying they never knew you proposed? Or that I said yes?"

He shook his head. "I only told Jesse. After we broke up, I was too embarrassed and hurt to tell the rest of my family. I just said we'd gone our separate ways. I couldn't get past my wounded pride."

Valerie blinked, and the missing piece of the puzzle clicked into place. Now she understood why Evan had asked her to keep their past quiet. Letting that sink in, she realized they each had their own reasons for leaving their past behind them.

"Evan?" She reached out and touched the back of his hand, grabbing his attention. "We needed to go our separate ways. We weren't ready to be married." Valerie spoke the words gently, wanting to comfort their younger selves, and possibly bridge the gap to their present situation. Neither one of them deserved to hold on to regret. Their paths may not have been perfect, but their decisions shaped them into the people they were today. Neither one of them had to be sorry about that.

Evan tipped his head at her, offering a one-sided grin. "We weren't." They shared a look of understanding, highlighted by the yellow moon and scattered stars. Valerie's heart lightened, and the tension between them melted.

Just then, Evan reached up and brushed his fingers across her cheek, causing her heart to skip a few beats. Her gaze flicked to his lips, which were parted. Was Evan going to kiss her?

"Mosquito," he said, and Valerie swallowed, realizing how ridiculous her assumption had been. He'd simply been saving her from a bug bite.

"Thanks." She released a breath and cocked her head, which tossed a strand of hair across her face. She was just about to push it back when Evan did it for her.

His fingers curled, looking restless, before he reached up and pushed the rogue strand of hair from her eyes. His rough fingertips moved slowly—with intention—across her forehead. When he tucked her hair behind her ear, Valerie shivered, not able to hide how he'd affected her.

"I—" she started, though she had absolutely no idea what she wanted to say. Her lungs ached to suck in a breath, but the only organ working was her heart—and it was beating faster by the second.

"I'm glad you came to dinner tonight." Evan's voice was gentle but held a rasp. It tethered her in place. "And that you ended up here. With me."

"Me too," she replied, almost involuntarily, and Evan's fingers found the edge of her jaw. They lightly caressed a line straight to her lips. Then, with the pad of his thumb, he brushed her parted mouth, watching her reaction as his featherlight touch teased her.

"I want to kiss you." His statement was confident, yet he didn't move an inch.

Valerie's breath hitched, realizing she wanted the same thing. Easing forward, she placed a hand on his jean-clad thigh, giving Evan silent permission to kiss her. Anticipation crackled between them. Tingles danced across her skin. And when their lips met, Evan instinctively curved his hand around her neck. He wove his fingers into her hair, and Val closed her eyes, surrendering to the moment. A swarm of butterflies exploded in her belly and flocked straight to her head.

Evan's earthy, intense scent was familiar yet new, acting as a switch that flicked her mind between past and present. But there was no mistaking the Evan she once knew with the man that held her now. Every touch, every move he made was deliberate and artfully controlled. His lips moved in perfect harmony with hers, entrancing her with his touch. This man knew exactly what he was doing, and he was driving her heart into a gear she wasn't used to, or maybe not ready for.

Valerie pressed into him, and Evan reciprocated, deepening their kiss. She wanted more—of the kiss, and of Evan—and the thought tightened around her, cutting off her air. She stiffened and Evan pulled back, concern in his eyes.

"Are you okay?" He continued to hold her, one hand woven into her hair.

She wasn't sure. Fear had mixed with want, and she suddenly wondered what she was doing. Was kissing Evan a good idea? In another week, she'd be back in California, or possibly filming in another location.

"I—" she breathed. "I don't think we should do this." Evan's gaze pinballed around hers until she slid her hand from his chest. "Our lives are still on different paths." She didn't want to start something that couldn't work. They'd have the same problem they'd had years ago.

Desire slid from his face, and she almost snatched her words back. Releasing his hold on her, Evan pressed his lips together. "You're right."

She didn't want to be. "I should go." She placed her hands in her lap.

"I'll walk you back," he offered, moonlight emphasizing every hard line that had just been pressed against her.

"I appreciate that, but I think I'll walk alone." She needed time to process everything that had just happened. How long had they been kissing? It had been both an eternity and a mere moment. She took a breath, wanting to steady her racing heart.

A frown hindered his handsome features. "Can I drive you?"

"I need the walk."

He nodded. "Can I at least put my number in your phone so you can text me when you get back to The Carriage House?"

Alarm bells sounded in Valerie's head, but she still removed her phone from her pocket and handed it to him. "If that will keep you from worrying."

"It will." He took her phone and plugged in his number before they both stood from the tailgate.

Valerie took her device back, internally battling herself. Stay and kiss him? Turn and run? It would be easy to ignore common sense and drift into him, letting his arms and lips find her again. "Good night, Evan."

"Good night, Val," he said, and she forced herself to walk away.

As she neared the trees, an irresistible pull tugged at her heart and she glanced back at Evan. He was still watching her, leaning against his truck, his arms crossed tightly over his chest. Vulnerability and need flickered across his face, a mirror to the emotion swirling within her. But she couldn't ignore the voice of caution echoing through her head. In an act of self-preservation, she looked away and forged ahead.

Chapter Twelve

Evan parked his truck in his parents' shed and made his way to the house. In the dark kitchen, he stopped to look at his phone once again. Val had surely made it back to The Carriage House safely, but she hadn't texted him yet, and he was worrying. He wanted to drive over and check on her, but understood that she needed some space. Just as he was about to call her, his phone lit up and dinged with a message.

Val: I made it safely to my room. No werewolf or vampire encounters. By the way, this is Val.

Evan grinned at her sarcasm, and found it endearing that she needed to clarify that it was her texting. As if he'd receive a text from some random number at this hour of the night. He typed out a quick response.

Evan: Good to hear. Though I was more worried about the bears. They eat at night.

Three dots appeared and then disappeared. A few seconds later, she was typing again.

Val: Really? I just took a stroll through bear infested woods?

He considered telling her that there were black bears in the area, but they mostly stayed away from people. It had been years since one had wandered close to town. Instead, he prodded her a little more.

Evan: If you ever see a bear, pretend you're a local. They especially like to eat Californians.

Val: Ha ha. Funny guy.

Evan replied with a winking emoji. A wide grin settled on his face.

"Dad?" Issy's voice startled him, and Evan jumped. His gaze jerked up from his phone to find his daughter's shadowy form in the archway between the kitchen and the living room. She flicked on the light. "What are you doing?"

For a second, there was a strange role reversal and Evan panicked, like she'd caught him sneaking in after curfew. He'd done that many times in his teenage years, though he and Jesse had usually climbed back in through their bedroom window. The big oak tree just outside their shared room kept most of their adventures a secret.

"Just texting Val." The words slipped out of his mouth before he really considered them.

"You're texting Val? *Now*?" Issy shifted the knitted blanket slung over her shoulders. Her surprise switched to curiosity. "What about?"

"I, uh—" Evan started, drawing a blank. He wasn't about to tell Issy he'd just been getting reacquainted with Val in the back of his truck. "I had an idea for the upstairs bathroom that I wanted to ask her about." His explanation sounded strange, even to his own ears.

Issy scrunched her brow. The messy bun on top of her head wobbled as she tilted her head. "And that was funny?"

"What?"

"You were texting her something funny about the bathroom?"

"I don't think . . ." Evan trailed off, not sure how he ended up being investigated by his daughter.

"Her text made you do this weird, goofy thing with your face." She quirked an eyebrow and smirked, prodding for the truth. Then her own phone brightened and dinged. She held it along with the blanket she wore like a cape, and the phone illuminated her face, which quickly went solemn. Her gaze bounced from Evan to the phone and back.

Evan went into dad mode. "Who are *you* texting, little missy?" He pointed at her with his phone, the tension in his chest lessening at the redirection of the hot seat.

Issy's mouth opened, but it took a few seconds for a response to come. "Kieffer."

"Kieffer Sanderson?" He'd been hoping for Amanda or Kayla, her two best friends. Not the cocky quarterback who found every excuse to take his shirt off and flaunt his muscles. "Why is he texting you at this hour?" Evan's back straightened, prickles of protectiveness winding his spine. He knew exactly what was on the mind of a teenage boy at this time of night.

Issy pursed her lips. "Actually, he asked me out."

"Details?"

"For dinner at The Silver Saddle. On Friday. Seven o'clock. Is that okay?"

Evan chewed his lower lip, processing. The Silver Saddle was a bar and grill on the edge of town. He knew everyone that worked there and would probably know everyone eating there. Fridays usually had a band of some sort and all-you-can-eat fish and chips. If Issy was intent on going on a date with shirtless quarterback guy, that was a good place for her to go.

"Home by eleven and don't let him take you anywhere else." Evan would put in a call to Luke, the manager, for an extra set of eyes.

Issy narrowed her gaze. "Dad, he's a perfectly nice guy. He won't throw me over his shoulder like a caveman and take me somewhere shady or something."

"Somewhere shady?" Just the idea set Evan on edge. "I'll remind him of how you should be treated when he picks you up."

"I know." Issy let out a long breath. "But that means I can go, right?" Her face brightened.

"Yes," he said, giving in. Kieffer wasn't a bad kid. He just wasn't the guy Evan would pick for his daughter to date. And he better keep every piece of clothing on in her presence.

"Okay!" Issy bounced on her bare feet and immediately zoned in on her phone, tapping away. When she was done, she looked up and gave Evan a smile. "I let Kieffer know he can pick me up at six-thirty and that you'd like to talk with him before we go to dinner."

Evan nodded and set his own phone on the kitchen island. "Tell him I'll be waiting with bells on."

"I will *not* tell him that." Issy smirked sweetly and winked before spinning on her heels. "Night, Dad. Love you."

"Night, sweetie. Love you too," he called after her, wishing he could slow down time. Maybe even rewind it? How had she grown up so fast?

Evan's phone dinged, and he peeked over to see that Val had replied.

Val: Glad we got to talk tonight.

He was about to reply when Issy called out from the stairwell, "Tell Val I said good night, too!"

Evan shook his head and grinned. Then he typed out a reply.

Evan: Me too. Sweet dreams.

The next morning, Evan stood in his house. It had been stripped clean and washed out—in a good way. The newly exposed wood floors were sanded and swept, running the length of the house like a golden airstrip. Every ounce of green and gold wallpaper had been removed, and the walls were being primed for paint. The new arch between the living room and kitchen framed the open space, showing it off, and Evan smiled. His house was shining up like a new penny.

In the kitchen, Issy and his mom were talking with Sasha, gathered around the new butcher block island. They were enjoying donuts, but kept giving Evan conspiring glances. He hoped they were talking about baked goods, but Evan knew better. Issy had probably run straight to his mom this morning to deliver the news that Evan and Val had been texting late last night. He could practically see the matchmaking gears turning in their heads. The only one not conspiring was Skippy—who sat attentively at Issy's feet, hoping for a donut crumb.

Evan shook his head, knowing their meddling was inevitable at this point. He'd shown the slightest bit of interest in Val, and now his mom and daughter were honing in. It was a good thing they didn't understand the extent of his interest in Val.

Last night, he realized there'd been a fire lying dormant inside him for years—since he'd last seen Val. He'd tried to ignore it, snuff it out, and extinguish it, but a spark had flickered when Val walked back into his life. It hit embers and was now a flame. When they'd kissed, heat had singed the inside of his chest, confirming he was in trouble. If Val hadn't pulled back, he could've kissed her all night. As it was, he couldn't stop thinking about how she'd melted perfectly into his arms.

But Val had a point. Their lives were still on different paths. He was firmly rooted in Maple Bay with his family. She had her own TV show. Her life played out in front of cameras and in magazines. Even if they started something while she was in town, what did that mean? He couldn't do a long-distance relationship again. Not at this point in his life.

Focusing elsewhere, Evan grabbed a bundle of rags and walked over to the fireplace. He handed one to Sal, who was halfway up a ladder. "Here you go." Sal thanked him and Evan set the remaining rags on the hearth, taking one for himself.

Dipping a brush into the bucket of watered-down white paint, Evan swiped the solution on the fireplace brick. After hitting every nook and cranny, he dabbed the surface with a rag, finishing the whitewashing technique. As he and Sal gave the fireplace a facelift, Val was putting a coat of stain on the stairs. Talking to the camera closest to her, she explained what she was doing, and Evan had a hard time focusing on anything outside of her voice.

"Can you believe how beautiful this is turning out?" she asked. "Yesterday we sanded and scraped the stairs and banister, bringing the wood back to its original state. Now we're staining the staircase." Val ran a wet brush across a step, completing a few strokes before smiling widely at the camera. "Look at that dark, rich color. It brings out the depth of the woodgrain and I can only imagine how gorgeous this is going to look after it's sealed and glossy."

Val continued and Evan didn't realize she'd entranced him until someone snatched the paintbrush from his hand.

"What the?" Evan looked down at his empty hand. The palm had a smear of slobber across it.

"Skippy! No!" Issy called from the kitchen, but Skippy was having too much fun to listen. The dog bounced about, showcasing the toy he'd retrieved—a wet paintbrush which was now dripping white paint on the sanded floor.

"Oh, no." Evan moved toward Skippy. "Come here, boy." He patted his thigh, trying to entice the pup close, but Skippy pranced a circle and shook his head, spraying paint like a sprinkler. It shot across the floor and splattered the newly stained stairs. Val squeak-gasped and Evan lurched forward, trying to grab the brush from Skippy's mouth. That instigated a chase. The pup galloped away from Evan, his nails clicking against the floor. Holding his head high to show off his prize, he ran through the half-open door that led to the basement, painting a streak on the frame as he escaped.

"Skippy, come!" Evan chased after him. All his furniture had been moved to the basement and Evan scrambled down the stairs, hoping to keep it from getting dog graffitied. Losing his footing on the last step, Evan caught the handrail, barely stopping himself from tumbling to the concrete floor.

"Sit! Stay!" Evan tried all the commands again, but he hadn't worked on the pup's training since he brought him home. Maybe Issy had taught him a trick or two? Other than how to snuggle?

Skippy raced a circle around the couch, and Evan sighed, knowing it wasn't the dog's fault that he didn't have manners. He'd been a stray and Evan knew nothing about his background, though he vowed to spend more time working with him after the renovation was done. "Stop!" Evan held up a hand. That got the pup's attention. He halted, but looked like he was waiting for the chase to start again.

Stuck in a standoff, Evan tried, "Drop it."

The pup held tight to the handle of the brush, his eyes wide in anticipation, especially when feet bound down the stairs behind Evan. They stopped halfway down.

"You want a piece of bacon?" Val asked, her voice pitched much higher than normal.

To Evan's surprise, Skippy dropped the brush and obediently sat, cocking his head like he was considering her question. Taking advantage of the pup's distraction, Evan snatched up the brush.

He breathed a sigh of relief, amazed his furniture hadn't been painted.

"Good boy." Evan scratched the pup's head, even though he wanted to tell him he was a little stinker. Still, dropping the brush deserved praise.

As he pet Skippy, Evan looked over his shoulder. Val was on the stairs, frozen mid-run, with a hand on the railing. A cameraman was behind her, still filming. Issy stood at the top of the stairs, mouthing the word "Sorry." Nina, Sasha, and Sal surrounded her.

The corner of Val's mouth turned up into a smirk. "Skippy sure knows how to get our attention, doesn't he?"

"Maybe not in the best way." Evan scoffed. "Are the stairs and floor salvageable?"

"They're fine." Val came down a few steps. "Nothing we can't fix."

Struck by the random question that stopped the chaos, Evan asked, "What made you think to ask him about bacon?" As soon as "bacon" left Evan's lips, Skippy sat up like a circus dog, balancing on his hind end. "Well, I'll be. Did we find the magic word?"

The pup gave a whine but stayed in his trick pose. Evan smiled. "I wish I had some bacon." He looked up the stairs at Issy. "Call Skippy, and get him a treat, please."

Issy whistled, and Skippy disappeared up the stairs, zigzagging past Val and the cameraman.

"My neighbor." Val joined Evan in the basement. "The one I pet-sit for. She feeds her cat a half-strip of bacon every day."

Evan quirked a brow. "I'm not sure that's good for a cat."

"It's probably not, but her cat's twenty-three years old, so she's got to be doing something right."

"Twenty-three? Wow. Maybe I should eat bacon every day?"

Val smiled, and Evan wished they were alone again. He wanted to pull her close, even though he knew it wasn't the best idea. Evan glanced at the cameraman, reminding himself not to make any rash decisions. It was probably good that they were filming.

Sliding her hands in her jean pockets, Val looked around. "Would you like us to do anything down here? Maybe some extra shelving?"

"Nah." His basement was an open cinderblock room that held all the odds and ends that didn't fit anywhere else. "I can build more shelves. I'd rather you focus on the parts of the house Issy and I actually live in."

Val nodded, but her eyes fell on something past the furniture. "Is that what I think it is?"

Evan turned, following her gaze, hoping there wasn't something embarrassing sticking out of a box he hadn't opened in years. His awkward middle school pictures still resided at his parent's house, so at least he didn't have to worry about those. "What are you looking at?"

Val navigated between the couch and stacked boxes, leading him to the wooden porch swing. "This would be perfect on your front porch." She set her hand on the swing, her green eyes sparkling with ideas. "Can I refinish it for you? Hang it with some twisted rope and add some pretty pillows? Where'd you get it?"

All her questions came out in a single breath, but Evan focused on the last. "It was my grandma and grandpa's porch swing."

"Oh." Her eyes went round and uncertain. "Are your grandparents still with you?"

He nodded. "My Grandpa Vern is, but my Grandma Barb passed quite a few years ago."

"I'm sorry to hear that."

"Thank you." He smiled, softly. "She was an amazing lady, and I'm blessed to still have my grandpa. He's in his nineties and as spry as they come. Still lives on his own in town, just a few blocks from my aunt Judy and cousin Myra. You'll have to meet him while you're in town. He's a hoot."

The wrinkles in her forehead relaxed. "I'd love to."

"This swing is from their farmhouse." Evan ran his gaze over the wooden slats and peeling paint. His childhood was filled with memories of summer evenings on the farm. Playing tag with his siblings. Sipping lemonade on the front porch. Watching the sun set over corn fields. But the memory of his grandpa and grandma on the swing was something he held close to his heart. During the summer months, they ended every evening on the porch swing—sitting together, holding hands, and enjoying their family. Their love was admirable and contagious. A love that had lasted the ages until his grandma took her last breath. Actually, it had lasted far beyond that. She was still here in spirit and his grandpa kept her memory alive, smiling like a teenager in love every time her name passed his lips. He visited her grave every Sunday, bringing her flowers and telling her about his week. It was a standing date he had with "his Barbie."

"We don't have to refinish it," Val said, catching his attention.

Evan looked up, wondering if his thoughts had played across his face. "I'd like to hang it on my porch someday. I'm just not sure I'm ready to right now."

Evan wanted to do the swing justice, to honor the example his grandparents had set for him. He wanted to share the swing with the woman who'd be his forever love. Someone who would stick with him through the thick and thin of life. At one time, he'd thought that would be Val. Then he'd wanted it to be Issy's mother. Both times he'd been wrong.

"I understand." Val's hand slid from the swing. She laced her fingers together in front of her waist. "I didn't mean to pry."

"You didn't." He might have expanded on his thoughts if the camera hadn't been looming in the distance. He could even imagine sharing the swing with Val if their lives found the same path. "For now, I'd like to stick with my rocking chairs."

She nodded. "Rocking chairs, it is."

But maybe one day, he'd be blessed to sit on this swing with the woman he loved.

Chapter Thirteen

Valerie leaned against the fence, looking out over the horse pasture as her phone rang. Her sister picked up just as the call was about to go to voicemail.

"Hey, sis," Gigi greeted. Her heels clipped in the background.

"Hey, sissy," Valerie replied. "You still at work?" It was after six, but Gigi often worked late in the evening. Valerie worried about her little sister putting in such long hours, but couldn't protest too much. She and her sister were self-proclaimed workaholics.

"Just leaving the office." Gigi gave a breathy sigh.

"Everything okay?"

Valerie and Gigi were two years apart in age, but Valerie had always felt maternal toward her sister, even when they were little girls. Without their dad in the picture, it was often just the two of them when their mom was working. Valerie was a decent cook before she hit middle school and managed a lot of the household chores, so their mom didn't have to stay up late washing clothes or dishes. It had been hard. Valerie had been jealous of classmates that had parents who picked them up after school or packed their lunches. But now, she was grateful for her work ethic and the close relationship she had with her sister.

"Everything's okay. I think," Gigi replied, the sounds of Chicago clattering in the background. Cars honked. A passing train rattled. "It's just that I've heard a lot of chatter around the office lately that the oldest Ryan son might be coming back to work for his dad."

"Really? How come?"

Gigi worked for a family-owned company that produced economical skin care products, and she'd been killing herself for the last few years to grow a new division within the company—an all-natural premium line specifically for women. The products were fabulous. Valerie could vouch for them. She'd converted her makeup bag to Gigi's product line.

"I'm not really sure." There was apprehension in Gigi's tone. Immediately, Valerie didn't like this guy.

"Oh, no. Have you worked with him before? What do we know about this guy?"

"I haven't worked with him. He actually hasn't worked for the company in more than a decade and I heard he left on bad terms."

"Like what?"

"I've heard all kinds of reasons why he left. Embezzlement. Ran off with his secretary. Went on a bender in Vegas. Gossip is flying around the office like a flock of hungry seagulls. I'm not sure what's true but none of it sounds good."

"Ugh. I'm sorry. I hope he's not a royal pain."

"Me too. I've got so many projects going right now and SheTime is finally pointed in the right direction. I don't need some high and mighty guy swooping in and messing it all up." Another horn honked in the distance, and Gigi sighed. "I'll let you know what happens. But more importantly, how's filming going?" Her sister's voice lightened with her question.

"Good." Valerie paused, considering her time with Evan. The ice cream. Dinner with his family. The kiss that had somersaulted her insides. "Better than good, actually."

"That's great! Not going to lie, I was a little worried when you said you'd be working on your ex-fiancé's house."

"Me too." Valerie picked at the edge of the wooden board with her thumb.

"That breakup was so hard on you."

Valerie set a boot on the fence, remembering how she'd leaned on her sister after ending the relationship with Evan. It had been one of the few times in her life when she'd fully broken down and let someone else take the wheel. Gigi came and stayed with her in L.A. for a month, making sure she ate and showered.

"I know," Valerie replied, not wanting to go to that place ever again. "But you don't have to worry anymore. All is good here. The renovation is coming along beautifully. We've got a ton of great footage for the pilot. Plus, Evan and I are getting along just fine, like old friends." If friends made your whole body hum with a single touch.

Valerie's mind shot back to last night, and a shiver cascaded up her spine.

"Good to hear," Gigi breathed, her heels clipping quicker. "You guys talked then? Did you ask him about what happened at the hospital?"

Valerie stiffened at the mention of her impromptu trip back to Minnesota. Her boot slid from the fence and back to the grass. "We talked, but I didn't ask him about that." Was there any sense in talking about it now? Evan had moved on quickly after their breakup. She hadn't. Her visit to the hospital had confirmed those two facts. It also spurred her back to California and forced her into her studies, where she always knew what to expect. In school, if she put effort in, she got results. She could say the same for work. However, that hadn't been her experience with love. "No sense in bringing that up now."

"Yeah, I guess." Gigi did not sound convinced, but before Valerie could squelch her sister's suggestion, she noticed Evan and Issy riding toward her. They were trotting their horses down the pathway between the two pastures.

"Hey, sissy. Can I call you back later? I've got something I need to take care of."

"Yeah, of course," Gigi said. "I'll be at Yappy Hour until about nine, so any time after that."

Valerie grinned at the term Gigi and her friends used for their evening get-togethers, which were a mix of happy hour, laughter, and plenty of conversation. *Yappy Hour.* "Enjoy, and tell the girls 'hi' from me."

"Will do. Alice is teaching Paige and I to knit. You should see the pitiful potholder I'm working on." Gigi huffed a chuckle.

"You're knitting?" Valerie almost looked at her phone to make sure she was still talking to her sister.

"Kind of. I'm not very good at it, but it's actually really relaxing."

"Huh," Valerie said, surprised but also thankful her sister was trying out a new hobby. It wasn't good for her to focus on work all day long. She needed something to slow her down. "Actually, that sounds fun."

"I'll make you a scarf for Christmas. I can't promise it'll be pretty, but I will knit it with love." Gigi paused. "And margaritas."

Valerie laughed. "I can't wait to wear it."

As she and her sister said their goodbyes, Evan and Issy approached, stopping their horses at the edge of the pasture.

"Hey, Val!" Issy waved from the saddle. Valerie waved back and walked over.

"Are you guys still filming?" Evan asked, looking from Valerie to the crew that wandered between the house and trailers.

Dang, he looked good on a horse. Rugged. Strong. Untamed. Her insides sighed. Who knew she had a thing for cowboys? Or maybe it was just this cowboy?

"Just got done." Valerie laced her thumbs in her jean pockets. "We were filming some B-roll footage to use for transitions."

"So, you're free now?" Issy asked, and Valerie nodded. "Good! Then you can ride Chico." Before Valerie knew what was happening, Issy dismounted.

"What?" Valerie stiffened.

"I got a call from Lilah while we were riding. She just got a momma goat and four newborn babies at the rescue." Issy walked toward Valerie. The horse followed. "The momma is having trouble nursing her kids, so Lilah needs help bottle feeding. I told her I'd be there as soon as I could."

"Oh." Valerie removed her thumbs from her pockets, and Issy set the leather reins in her hands.

"If you could ride Chico, then I can head over to Lilah's now." Issy's face was bright, probably thinking of the baby goats she couldn't wait to snuggle. "And help the babies."

Valerie couldn't say no to that. "I guess I could, but I haven't ridden since I was a kid."

"Great!" Issy's smile went into megawatt mode. "Chico is such a good boy. He'll take care of you. You don't have to worry about a thing." She patted Chico on the neck and then kissed his nose. He stood there like he was used to the attention.

Valerie glanced up at Evan, not sure what she'd gotten herself into.

"It'll be a short trail ride. I'm getting this colt used to riding outside of the arena, and it gives Pistol confidence to be with a seasoned veteran. We'll just ride alongside the lake for a bit and go back to the barn." Evan nodded his head at Chico. "And Chico is about as seasoned as they get. If you can sit in a saddle, you'll be fine with Chico. He's bombproof."

Valerie paused. She was still uncertain, but her inner child had always wanted a pony, and that little girl took over. "I guess I should probably make use of these cowboy boots while I'm here." She rocked back on her heel and grinned.

"Definitely." Evan rubbed his horse's neck. "You need to break in those boots with some saddle time." He smiled, and Valerie appreciated how the creases around his lips had deepened over the years.

"I'll help you mount up." Issy took the reins back and draped them over Chico's neck. There was still a kernel of anxiety in Valerie's gut, but she put her boot in the stirrup before she could talk herself out of riding. Once she'd hoisted herself into the saddle and took hold of the reins, Issy stepped back and said, "You two kids have fun." She stretched the last word into a few syllables and gave her dad a mischievous wink.

Evan smirked and shook his head as his daughter walked off.

"What was that about?" Valerie asked, the kernel of anxiety bursting like popcorn. "You didn't put me on a wild mustang, did you?" Suddenly, the ground looked far away.

"No, it's nothing." Instead of answering her questions, Evan clucked his tongue. Both horses started walking.

Valerie gasped and grabbed the saddle horn as soon as Chico swayed beneath her.

"I promise you, Chico is safe," Evan said, and Valerie glanced at him. He rode next to her and in the saddle, they were the same height. Under the brim of his black cowboy hat, Valerie caught the confidence that came with his statement. "Do you trust me?"

His stare hit her core, easing it. She'd always trusted him, even when she'd fought her intuition. Evan was built different from most men in her life. He always tried to do the right thing.

"I do." She let her body relax—starting with her fingers.

"Good." He adjusted his hat. "Chico is Jesse's retired roping horse. He's the first horse Charlie rode."

"The first horse? Isn't Charlie like six years old?"

"We start 'em early around here." He smiled. "She was riding Chico by the time she was four."

"Really?" Valerie looked down at the chestnut horse. He was plodding along at a steady rhythm—opposite of Evan's horse, who had his golden neck arched, assessing his surroundings like a dragon. "Now I feel silly for doubting Mr. Chico."

Chico flicked an ear back, acknowledging her apology.

"He's the horse we start all the kids on. I'm sure Baby G will be in that saddle in a few short years."

It amazed Valerie that all the Westons shared a love for horses. "Did Issy start riding that young, too?"

"She did." Evan rubbed his horse's neck, whispering a few soothing words. "She started on my retired rodeo horse. He's the horse I learned to rope on as a teenager, if you can believe that."

Valerie did the math in her head. That seemed impossible, but Evan had started his family right after college. "That's really neat. I love that you passed your passion onto to her."

"We definitely share a strong love for animals, much to her mother's dismay."

Valerie got caught on his last sentence. "Her mom isn't an animal lover?"

Evan shook his head as they neared the edge of the lake. "Nah. Never was. That should have been my first red flag, but I ignored it."

She hummed an agreeable response, looking out over the smooth, sparkling water. "Sometimes it's hard to see the red flags. Love has a way of blinding you to them." She'd missed a sea of warnings with Ryker.

Sliding a glance at her, Evan looked to analyze her comment. "Tracy wasn't made for this place. I should've seen that. I tried to fit her into a world she wasn't made for."

Valerie wanted to know more. What wasn't she made for? "She didn't enjoy living here? In this little piece of heaven?"

"She didn't like small town life, or the horses and the lifestyle that comes with them. She wasn't happy. We tried to make it work. I wanted to keep our family together. We even considered moving back to Minneapolis before Issy started school, but we would've had the same problem there. She might've been happy, but I wouldn't have."

Hooves padded along the dirt path, and the sway of the saddle glided through her. "You really love this place, don't you?" She could see why. A loving family, the peace of the country, and the beauty of the horses surrounded him.

"Couldn't see myself living anywhere else."

Valerie nodded, contemplating the idea of settling down in a place like Maple Bay. She couldn't help but wonder if she would've been like Tracy if she'd moved here in her twenties and started a family. Would she have been restless for more? Maybe. Could she see herself living here now? Enjoying a simpler life? Also, maybe. The thought sent her stomach into a fluttery spin.

Valerie twisted in the saddle, pushing away her silly thoughts. Still, she couldn't help addressing something she'd found increasingly puzzling. How was this handsome, caring man single? Especially since it seemed like his mom was on a mission to find him a wife. "How come you're not dating anyone?"

Evan startled, and she almost took her question back.

After a pause, he said, "Dating in a small town is hard. My options are pretty slim. I've dated here and there, but nothing long term since Tracy and I split."

"Nobody's captured your heart since then? I don't believe it." She meant to be playful. If he'd been close, she might've given him a little nudge.

"Not until recently."

Her heart hiccupped and bounced against her ribs. Was he talking about her? The certainty in his ice-blue eyes stole her breath.

"I—" She was about to admit she was glad they'd reconnected, even if neither of them intended to do so, but two ducks shot out of a patch of cattails. As the birds overzealously flapped their wings and flew into the sky, Evan's horse burst into a frenzy. Pistol reared up, flailing his front legs before jumping sideways and dancing into a high step. Immediately, Valerie grabbed the saddle horn and squealed, bracing for a bone-jarring fall. But Chico simply watched the fiasco unfold.

Thankfully, Evan stuck to the saddle like glue, keeping his cool as his mount pranced beneath him. He talked to his horse and stroked its neck, calming the animal's panicked nerves. When all four hooves finally stayed on the ground, Valerie breathed a sigh of relief.

"That was amazing," she gasped, relaxing her grip on the saddle horn. "I can't believe you stayed on."

Evan smirked. "I've been through worse than that." He patted Pistol. "That's why I always bring Chico along. He's a calming influence on the young colts. Without him, things could've really gotten ugly."

Valerie looked down at Chico, admiring the horse's calm demeanor. His head was cocked, staring at Evan's horse like the rambunctious youngster he was. "You are the best horse ever. I think you deserve a treat. An apple? Carrots? Maybe cake? Whatever you like." She scratched his neck appreciatively.

Evan laughed. "I've got apples back at the barn. He definitely deserves a couple."

"Great. Do you have wine too?" Valerie asked, her adrenaline still pumping.

"For Chico?" Evan quirked a brow.

"No, for me," she replied, catching her breath. "I'm going to need a glass after that."

Evan's eyes lit up. "I think I can find a few glasses for us."

Chapter Fourteen

Back at the barn, Evan unsaddled the horses and Val helped brush them. She looked enamored with Chico, giving him affectionate scratches, two apples, and a few kisses.

"Chico and I would be happy to take you out on another trail ride whenever you'd like," Evan offered, hauling a saddle and pad toward the tack room.

"I might take you up on that." She brushed her fingers through Chico's forelock, and Evan grinned, more for himself than for the horse.

After the horses were in their stalls, he said, "I need to feed the horses their dinner, and then I promise I'll get you a glass of wine."

"Can I help?" Val walked over to Evan, where he was loading a bale of hay into a wheelbarrow.

"Sure." Grinning, Evan pushed the wheelbarrow down the aisle, delivering hay and grain to each stall. Val was eager to listen and help, asking curious questions as they navigated the barn.

"Do horses really sleep standing up?"

"Yes, they can lock their knees while they doze, but they lay down and sleep too."

"How did Pistol get his name?"

"He came into the world running and hasn't stopped since."

"What's the difference between a gelding and a stallion?"

The answer to that one made her blush and when they'd completed evening chores, Evan had a permanent smile on his face. It had taken triple the usual time to feed, but he didn't mind. It was nice to share his passion with Val and see the horses through her eyes.

"You ready for that glass of wine?" He brushed hay bits from his hands.

"Yes, please."

They walked the short distance to The Carriage House, meandering through tall oak trees. Once at the inn, Evan retrieved a bottle of chilled rosé and two stemless glasses from the kitchen. Then he joined Val on the stone patio, which sat on the back of the building and faced the lake.

"Quiet here tonight." Val leaned against the backside of an Adirondack chair and looked out over calm waters. "The crew must've gone out for drinks at The Silver Saddle. That's their new favorite spot."

Evan set the bottle and glasses on the patio table. "There's line dancing there tonight."

"Oh, boy." Val chuckled. "They'll probably be there until closing."

"It's a good time." Evan filled both glasses, glancing at Jesse and Hazel's house as he did. It didn't look like anyone was home. "Jesse and Hazel must be out making the rounds. Charlie has dance lessons a few times a week and Grace joined 4H this summer."

"They stay busy, huh?"

"They do." Setting the bottle down, he scanned the lush, sloping grass that led to the shoreline. The lake reflected ribbons of pink sky. "Looks like we have this view to ourselves." Which did not bother him in the least.

"Lucky us." Val tipped her chin to the sky and closed her eyes. Warm rays bathed her skin, illuminating the graceful curve of her neck and elegant line of her jaw. For a moment, she looked lost, part of the serene beauty that surrounded them. When her eyes opened, she turned to Evan with a content smile, forcing his chest to bound in a way he wasn't used to. "You get to enjoy this every day?"

He nodded, though every day was not like this. Val had made it sweeter.

"I think this view deserves a toast." He handed a glass to Val, not able to tear his gaze away from her.

"What should we toast to?"

"To evenings like these." He raised his glass, making Val's emerald eyes twinkle.

"To evenings like these," she repeated, before clinking her glass to his.

In the hush that followed, they took generous sips of the cool, crisp wine. Val's eyes closed with an appreciative hum, and Evan had to take another glug when she lightly ran her tongue over her bottom lip.

"This is perfect," she murmured, and took another drink. She kept her gaze intently on Evan, and the connection between them nearly yanked him forward. His pulse skittered.

"Especially on a scorching day like this," he said. Was it getting hotter?

Val pressed her mouth together, pausing. "I have to admit, I thought about jumping in the lake several times today. Actually, it's pretty tempting right now."

The alcohol might've gone straight to his head, but Evan couldn't think of a better way to end the night. Plus, the way his mind was wandering, he could use a brisk dip. "Let's do it."

"Jump in the lake?" She stopped short of another sip.

Evan set down his glass. "I'll race you there, but I highly suggest taking off your boots." He grabbed an Adirondack chair for balance and pulled off one cowboy boot and sock.

"Really?" Val laughed, like he couldn't be serious.

Popping off the second boot, he said, "They're a pain to swim in."

She cocked her head, questioning him, but the curious glint in her eye spurred him forward. Without another word, Evan jogged off toward the lake. Val laughed, and the sound sent a wave of warmth through him.

"I'm definitely winning this race," he shouted over his shoulder.

"I'm taking off my boots!" Val called back, making Evan grin wider. When he got to the shoreline, he glanced back. Val was running toward him.

"You better get out of my way!" she teased, and Evan lurched forward, setting foot on the warm, wooden slats of the dock. He ran down it like a diving board, yanking his T-shirt up and off. He tossed it behind him before swan diving into the lake, hoping Val didn't chicken out at the last second.

He wanted to share this with her.

Cool water enveloped him, making him weightless as he plunged into dark depths. The world above melted away. The rush of water drowned out all sounds except for the steady beat of his heart, which picked up when Val joined him.

Evan spun toward the muted splash, just in time to see her sail through the water like a mermaid. Dark hair rolled behind her, along with a trail of bubbles. Below the surface, it almost looked like she was dancing, every kick and stroke a deliberate move, capturing his attention until they both pushed toward the sky.

Breaking the surface, Evan sucked in a lungful of air, pure exhilaration shooting through him as Val laughed—wild and joyful. It made him want to scoop her up, haul her back to the patio, and do it all over again.

"Evan Weston," she scolded. His name bounced out of her mouth. "I can't believe you got me to jump in the lake!" She splashed him with her fingertips.

"Feels good, doesn't it?" He challenged, treading water. Val did the same, her arms butterflying out around her.

"It does." She smiled, wide and intent, holding his gaze before moving into an easy backstroke. Her fingers and toes rippled through the water, and Evan lazily swam beside her, letting all his cares wash away. A few minutes later, when they neared the dock, he grabbed hold of the ladder and reached out to Val. She turned to her stomach and took his hand, and Evan couldn't resist any longer. With a tug, he pulled Val close.

She glided toward him, her hands finding his shoulders and making waves in his heart. Sliding an arm around her waist, he aligned her soft curves to the hard plane of his chest. Val responded by wrapping her jean-clad legs around his middle, sending a ripple of water past them. Evan's pulse thrummed, and he kept their heads above water with a hand and foot balanced on the ladder.

"This was a good idea," Val whispered, merely inches from his mouth. A droplet of water dripped from the end of her nose.

"One of my best," he replied, making her emerald eyes dance.

"Thanks for the tip about the cowboy boots."

"Any time."

In the next breath, their lips met with a kiss that consumed Evan. Lightning ran up and down his spine, and he was certain the heat between them simmered the lake. The moment was surreal. He didn't think he'd ever hold Val again, but having her wrapped in his arms felt right, like maybe they'd always been meant for a second chance.

Val gave a breathy sigh, and he tightened his grip on her waist. When she ran her fingers through his hair, Evan considered scooping her up and carrying her onto the dock, where he could lay her on the sun-warmed boards. But he just couldn't let her go. Not for a second. Instead, he pressed a trail of kisses along her cheek, neck, and collarbone, savoring her sweet scent and wondering how long he could keep her close. Forever?

His heart kicked at the thought. Val's presence wasn't permanent, but holding her forced reality away, leaving only the electricity between them. Every touch, every kiss further confirmed their connection. And when Val eased back, he scanned her beautiful eyes, soaking in the desire that lingered.

She bit her swollen bottom lip, nearly making Evan's chest explode.

"I'm glad we have the lake all to ourselves," she said, and Evan grinned.

"Me too." He pushed a strand of hair from her face, and Val set her head on his shoulder, wet tresses trailing his bare chest.

"Finish that glass of wine with me?" she asked, her fingernails tracing his neck.

He wanted to stay there, wrapped up in her, but wouldn't tell her no. "You wait on the dock. I'll get our glasses."

She smiled against his neck before kissing it. He eased her toward the ladder, and Val climbed the rungs, water cascading from her clothes. He followed her.

Once on the dock, Evan swept a hand through his hair, pushing it back. Turning toward him, Val wrung out the front of her tank top, but stilled as her gaze trailed a heated blaze over his bare stomach and chest. He smirked, thoroughly enjoying the spark in her eyes. Until her energy dwindled, giving him pause.

"What's wrong?"

She stepped to him, letting go of the spiraled hem of her shirt. Reaching out, she ran her fingertips gently over his chest, but Evan couldn't get past the look on her face. It was as though she'd seen a ghost.

"Your scar," she whispered, still focused on his chest.

Briefly, he looked down to where she touched him—below his collarbone, where a few inches of skin held a permanent mark from his past. Memories of his surgery and the incident that preceded it were part of him as well. But like his scar, they'd faded and gotten less painful as time passed.

"It's where the doctors put my defibrillator," he explained, wanting to ease the worry etched on her face. "After my episode on the football field. When I went into cardiac arrest." He and Val hadn't been together when it happened, and Evan honestly wasn't sure if Val knew the details.

Her lashes fluttered. "You've been okay since?"

He nodded, reaching out to cup her elbow. "Never had another episode."

Her fingertips skimmed the line of rough skin, and Evan's mind went in reverse, to his collapse on the football field—or what he remembered of it.

It'd been a scorching summer day, the air thick with humidity. Lightheaded and exhausted, Evan refused to give any less than one hundred percent at practice. The NFL draft was a week away, and he couldn't afford to miss any opportunity to showcase his skills. Football had been his passion, his driving force through high school and college. He'd dreamt of playing professionally since he was little. And then, on that fateful day, his world came crashing down.

Evan vividly recalled sprinting down the field, pushing his body to its limit, when darkness suddenly engulfed him. The next thing he remembered was waking up on his back, a sea of concerned faces looking down at him. Later, he learned that his heart had stopped for nearly five minutes. Medics, with their swift response, had brought him back to life through CPR and an external defibrillator. It was a miracle he'd survived. However, that miracle came at a cost. His dream of a pro football career died that day. No NFL team wanted to take a chance on a kid with a heart problem. No matter how hard he'd worked, or that he'd never had any health issues until that day.

"The defibrillator monitors my heart and corrects the rhythm if there's a problem," he explained. It was the easiest way to sum up what had become a normal part of his life.

Val searched his eyes. "I'm glad that never happened to you again."

His heart quivered under her touch, reminding Evan that life could hand out tough, unexpected challenges. Yet, those challenges had shaped the wonderful life he had today. They led him to this very moment, giving him a connection he didn't know he needed.

Reaching up, he caressed Val's jaw with a finger. Standing there with her, soaked from their swim and dripping on the dock, Evan wanted to tell her how grateful he was that she'd come back into his life. There was a powerful urge to confess feelings that had reignited in her presence. Being around Val had reminded him of what he was missing—a partner to share his life with.

Val tipped her chin up, and he grazed the delicate curve of her neck. Her hand lay flat against his chest, directly over his heart. Evan was sure she felt it beating against her palm.

"I wish you would've let me see you that day," she said tenderly. "I understand why you didn't, but I wanted to make sure you were okay. Even though we weren't together, I still cared about you."

Evan stilled, his heartbeat echoing as he took in her words. "What day?"

She blinked at him, her head tilting. "The day of your surgery. At the hospital."

"You—" Evan paused and swallowed. "You came to see me when I was in the hospital?"

Her mouth parted. The corners of her eyes creased as she nodded. "You didn't know?"

He shook his head, almost involuntarily, as questions arose and crashed into each other. The world slowed, muffled by this information, like he was back underwater. "No."

The shock on Val's face mirrored his own. "I—" she stuttered. "I made it to the hospital just before you went into surgery."

And just like that, Evan was reminded of how one moment in time could alter the course of a life forever.

Chapter Fifteen

Valerie steadied herself, pressing into Evan's chest with her palm. He didn't know she'd been there? That she'd dropped everything when she heard he was in the hospital? Spent every cent she had to make it to his bedside before he went into surgery?

The truth of what had happened materialized and hit her.

"Ranae called me after you were taken to the hospital," she said, referring to a girlfriend of one of the football players, a woman Valerie had gotten to know while she and Evan had dated. "She told me what happened and where they took you. I booked a flight that same day."

Evan stepped back. "What?" His eyes were wide, unbelieving. "But I didn't . . . you didn't . . ."

"I went straight from the airport to the hospital," she breathed, a rock settling in her stomach. "I asked for you at the nurse's station and my voice must've carried through the lobby because Tracy approached me." Valerie could still picture the scene in her head, as if it were yesterday. Panic. Uncertainty. The starch, clinical scent. How she'd jumped when a stranger touched her.

"Can I help you?" The stranger had asked, her hand on Valerie's arm. Before Valerie replied, the woman gave her first name and introduced herself as Evan's girlfriend. The shock must've gone straight to Valerie's face, because Tracy quickly assessed her with a narrowed stare.

"Tracy?" Evan asked, referring to his ex-wife. His features were flat and motionless.

Valerie nodded. "I told her who I was and asked if I could see you."

He closed his eyes, running a hand up and down his face. "And what did she say?"

"That you didn't want to see me. Only family and friends were allowed. She said you and her were happy, and I should leave you alone," Valerie whispered, the gravity of that moment sinking in. "So, I left and went back to L.A."

Evan released a heavy sigh. Stunned, Valerie went slack, and her hand slipped from Evan's chest. The absence of his warmth gutted her, but Evan immediately grabbed her hand and brought it back to his chest. Their fingers intertwined, and he pressed her hand to his heart. Valerie's knuckles brushed against his scar.

"I would've never sent you away. She had no right to tell you that." His pale blue eyes pierced her, shattering a harsh memory she'd turned over in her head a million times.

Valerie's breath hitched. The weight of his words was too much to bear as they stood there, gripping each other, breathing in the truth. For so long, she'd believed Evan had pushed her away. That she'd been unwanted and easily replaced. Now, in this moment, the truth was sinking in and taking root. He hadn't even known she'd come for him.

"I was so worried about you," she said, tears pricking her eyes. Valerie blinked, forcing them away. "I was terrified something would happen to you during surgery. I had to see you . . . to make sure you knew how much I cared for you." In truth, she'd come to the hospital to tell Evan she still loved him. She'd walked away for the same reason.

Evan squeezed her hand. His chest rose and fell with deep breaths. "I don't know what would've happened if I'd seen you that day." His words were soft, laced with pain and conviction. "But I can tell you that after my surgery, I went on a difficult journey. I was depressed. Angry. I couldn't understand how my life could be flipped upside down by something outside my control. I hated my body for disowning me, and didn't know who I was anymore."

Valerie tightened her grip, physically feeling his pain. "I wish I could've been there for you."

He shook his head. "I'm glad you weren't."

Valerie startled, not expecting his response.

"I would've pulled you into that dark place with me." Concern clouded his eyes. "If I'd seen you at the hospital, I would've done everything in my power to reconcile and convince you to stay by my side. I didn't know better then."

Valerie was suddenly aware of her chest rising and falling with quick breaths. "What do you mean?"

"I would've done what was best for me, selfishly." He took a step closer, narrowing the gap between them. "Not what was best for you, or us."

A surge of emotions washed over Valerie. His words soothed an old wound on her heart, and in that moment, she was simply grateful for the choices they'd both made. Right or wrong, their choices had placed them here, gazes locked, holding onto each other like a wave might sweep in and steal them away.

She leaned into his grip. "If I'd seen you that day and you'd wanted to get back together, I would have." Valerie surprised herself with her confession. It shifted something inside her, changing her perception of their history. "But we both needed to go on our separate journeys." No matter how hard that had been.

"And I'm thankful those journeys brought us here," he replied, seeming to understand exactly what she was saying. "To this very moment."

Anticipation trailed up her spine, making her stand taller. "Me too."

They shared a smile, a silent agreement to let go of past decisions and pain. The years between them melted away, and Evan leaned in to kiss her, making Valerie forget everything except the present.

The next day Valerie worked hard to concentrate on the task at hand—putting a fresh coat of paint on Evan's house. But her head was foggy. Was it possible to have a kiss hangover? To have the sensations from last night still stuck in her brain? She'd told herself to focus on siding, trim, and camera angles, but her eyes had other ideas. They kept finding Evan, and each time his gaze caught hers, her stomach bottomed out. She spent the entire day pretending to think about gingerbread trim and exterior paint, but really, she was conspiring on how to see Evan again.

"So, *what* is going on between you and Evan?" Nina asked, during their drive back to the inn. She craned her neck and stared at Valerie like she'd been keeping the world's biggest secret. "*Spill. The. Tea.*"

"What? No." Valerie sputtered. Had her thoughts been that transparent? Stiffening, she scanned the back of the van, even though she and Nina were the only two in it. "Nothing happened between us. Nothing *is* happening between us." The correction gave Nina the confirmation she was looking for.

"You are the worst liar." Nina cocked an eyebrow and laughed. "You get this twitchy-blinky thing with your right eye when you try to lie, and that is definitely happening right now."

Valerie touched her face. It was doing something weird. Maybe she should wink when she lied? "What do you mean?" Her eye twitched again, and she gave up, dropping her hand to her lap.

"You and Evan are like magnets. There's this electric force field between you two that beams like a rainbow. It's hard to miss."

Valerie scoffed and sank back against the seat. "Quite the picture you're painting."

"It's accurate." Nina took her eyes off the road and shot Valerie a knowing look. "I thought there was chemistry right off the bat, especially when I watched some of the footage back, but it's been getting more and more obvious. Is there something you're not telling me? Been rekindling that spark with Mr. Greek-god-in-Wranglers?"

Valerie rolled her eyes, mainly to stop her eye from involuntarily twitching. Because Nina wasn't wrong. There was rekindling and reconsideration taking place, as Valerie was getting to know the remarkable man Evan had become.

Nina cleared her throat. "I'm dying over here! Spill the tea, please!"

With a sigh, Valerie met Nina's gaze, a mix of uncertainty and hope springing through her. "Maybe there's something there," she admitted. "Something I need to figure out."

"I knew it!"

Valerie smirked and let Nina spin for a few seconds before adding fuel to her fire. "And he definitely looks good in his Wranglers." The image of Evan standing on the dock flashed through her mind. Soaking jeans, bare chest, and a heated gaze like he was about to have his way with her. She sighed. "He should be their spokesperson."

Nina laughed and slapped the steering wheel. Her dark curls bounced. "So, are you going to do something about it, or just keep admiring him from afar?"

Valerie had already admired Evan up close—a few times—but she wanted to keep that information to herself. She shrugged. "I think I'll continue appreciating his chiseled features and steely eyes from a distance."

Nina made a noise like someone had gut-punched her. "Why from a distance? Life's too short for that!"

Valerie thumbed the edge of her seatbelt. "I don't want anything to get in the way of finishing this job and making the pilot the best it can be." Truthfully, she didn't want to get hurt again. Putting her heart on the line would only end in pain when she and Evan went their separate ways.

"Val, everything is going amazing." Nina parked the van next to The Carriage House and turned off the engine. "We have so much great footage and you're killing it as a host. I shared a few pieces with Tom and he loves it."

"He *loves* it?" Valerie grabbed hold of the seatbelt to ground herself. Tom was a harsh critic. "He actually said the word 'love'?"

Nina cocked her head. "Well, it was more like 'this is way better than I thought it was going to be.' But that's basically an A+ rating from Tom."

Valerie blinked. It was.

"And he wants to talk more about our idea for the show on historical buildings. He already booked a meeting for us next week."

Valerie sat straight up and looked at Nina. "He did?!"

"He did." Nina's smile widened. "He called about an hour ago. I've been dying to tell you."

Valerie's mouth hung open. She was stunned, elated, and perplexed at the same time. This is what she wanted—a chance to redeem herself and the option to secure her own series on HomeTV. But despite the wonderful news, there was a part of her that wasn't excited.

"Wow, that's great," she said, ignoring the uncertainty hiding in her gut.

"My point is, everything is going as planned with filming," Nina continued, "And you're allowed to have some fun. Life isn't *all* about work. So, go on a date. Kiss the cowboy."

Valerie's mind shot back to Evan. She pursed her lips, pondering the kisses they'd already shared and the way he made her feel—desired, wanted, valued. "Maybe," she replied.

"Kiss him."

"We'll see."

Nina opened the door. "You better not wait too long to kiss that cowboy." She quirked her brow. "There's only a few days left of filming."

Valerie was sure Nina's reminder was a friendly push, but her words sent Valerie into a spin. As they went into the inn, Valerie's thoughts raced, consumed by a ticking clock. *Two days.* That's all she had left with Evan before returning to L.A. What did she truly want from him? Was she ready for something more?

By the time the sun set, Valerie had turned over countless scenarios in her head, but one thing was clear. She couldn't afford to waste any time. While she was here, Valerie was determined to make every moment count.

Chapter Sixteen

Standing in his backyard, Evan admired the crisp coat of ivory paint that brightened his home. He'd been resistant to the cranberry trim but had put his faith in Val and loved the way it turned out. The dark cranberry contrasted perfectly with the white, showcasing the intricacies of the gables, eaves, and window frames. It was picture-perfect, looking like a home straight from the pages of a storybook.

"Come on, Skippy," Evan called. The pup romped over from the willow tree, where he'd been chasing the ends of wispy branches as they danced in the breeze. "Cats are all fed."

Evan had made sure his five feisty felines had plenty of food in the shed. They had their own cat door, plush beds, and could come and go as they pleased, but they'd mostly kept to the shed this past week and away from all the commotion. After giving them plenty of scratches, he promised that the chaos and construction would stop soon.

Back at the house, he opened the door and called out to Issy. "You said Kieffer is going to pick you up at six-thirty?" He entered the kitchen with Skippy on his heels, expecting to find Issy where he'd left her—sitting on a barstool at their butcher block island, fiddling with the design program on Val's laptop.

Issy was still in the same spot, but to Evan's surprise, Val stood next to her.

"He should be here any minute," Issy replied cheerily. "Look who stopped over."

Evan paused, his hand still on the doorknob. Val gave him a tentative smile and waved.

"Hey," he breathed, a rush of excitement zipping through him. "What are you up to?" He should have said *nice to see you* or *'I was going to call you.'* He could've even told Val that he couldn't stop thinking of her. But none of those things left his mouth.

"I brought wallpaper samples for Issy to look at," Val replied, alerting Skippy to her presence. He raced around the island, and Val bent to pat his wiggly body.

"Aren't they gorgeous?" Issy stared at the butcher block where a dozen square pieces of patterned paper were fanned out.

Val continued to rub Skippy. His tail thumped against the cabinets. "I ordered them from a décor store in Bemidji," Val explained. "Sasha picked them up today, and I thought I'd stop over to see which one Issy liked best for her bedroom. I stopped at your parents' place and they said you were here. Your dad gave me a ride over."

"Oh," Evan replied, wishing she'd stopped over for more than wallpaper.

"I love them all." Issy placed her elbows on the wood, staring at the wallpaper samples as if she had an impossible decision ahead of her. "Which is your favorite, Val?"

Val leaned over the options, tapping her finger to her chin. Evan closed the door and walked to the island, smiling at the sight of Issy and Val. They were standing side by side, lost in thoughts of colors, hues, and patterns.

Val touched a floral design in shades of bright pink and green. "This one is bold. It'd work best on an accent wall."

Issy nodded. "Yeah. I could totally see that. Maybe the wall behind my headboard?"

Val made an agreeable noise. "Yes, and this one is more subdued." She pointed to a soft blue paisley pattern. "It reminds me of the scarf you showed me at the feed store. The one I had to have, even though I have no need for a scarf anytime soon. Especially with this heat."

Issy grinned, keeping her eyes on the samples. "It totally looks like the scarf." She smiled at Val, making Evan's heart squeeze. "Which one do you like best, Dad?"

"Whatever you like, sweetie. I don't think you can go wrong with any of these choices."

Issy nodded, just as there was a knock at the door. "That's Kieffer." She jolted up and hopped off the barstool. "Can we talk more about the wallpaper in the morning?"

"Of course," Val said. "We'll chat then and once you pick out your favorite, I'll get it ordered and picked up so we can install it the next day."

"Thank you!" Issy hopped toward Val, surprising her with a hug. Val quickly melted into the embrace.

"You're welcome."

Hurrying off, Issy left Evan and Val in the kitchen, staring at each other over butcher block and wallpaper. Evan tipped his head toward the front of the house, where the door squeaked open, and a male voice carried through to the kitchen.

"She's got a date tonight," he explained.

Val grinned, putting her hands in her back pockets. "She told me. They're going to dinner at The Silver Saddle?"

Evan nodded and pursed his lips. "And I need to put the fear of God in him before he drives off with my daughter. Can you excuse me for a few minutes?"

Val seemed entertained. "Go take care of business."

Reluctantly, Evan headed toward the front door. Mostly, he was dreading the idea of his daughter going on a date with Mr. Shirtless Quarterback. But Evan also didn't want to leave Val. If she'd only come to drop off wallpaper samples, could he convince her to stick around once Issy left? Would she spend another evening with him?

After a five-minute conversation with Issy and her date, Evan laid down his rules and was satisfied with how he'd made Kieffer squirm. Convinced his daughter would be returned safely and on time—or else—Evan waved goodbye, and the kids drove off, slowly.

As he headed back inside, Evan considered what it would be like to take Val on a proper date. But Maple Bay didn't have Michelin Star restaurants or art museums. It was nothing like L.A. Would Val be happy getting a burger at Jake's? A root beer float at the drive-in? Having a picnic near the lake? Evan strode through the empty living room with a head full of questions, but a sweet scent tickled his nose and distracted him from his thoughts. Looking ahead, he spotted Val hovering near the oven.

"What's that smell?" Evan navigated around the island.

Val gave him a one-sided smile. She had two frilly potholders in her hands—which had definitely come from his mom's kitchen. "When I stopped at your parents' house looking for you and Issy, your mom was baking. She was testing out recipes for the pie baking contest later this summer and insisted I take a pie to share with you and Issy." She shrugged. "I couldn't resist."

Evan leaned against the counter, grateful for a reason to spend more time with Val. "Understandable. My mom's pies are irresistible. Especially if she was working on perfecting her apple pie recipe for Maple Bay Days."

Val's eyes widened. "Yes, that's *exactly* what she was doing." She opened the door of his fancy new oven, exposing a bubbling apple pie. The scent of warm cinnamon and sugar wafted through the kitchen as Val removed the pie and carefully set it on the counter. "She gave us the Caramel Apple Pie and said she wanted to hear our thoughts on it in the morning."

Steam rose in curls from the crumbly topping, and Evan's stomach rumbled. "That's my favorite recipe of hers. I don't know what she could do to make it any better. It's this perfect combination of a pie and a crisp." Suddenly, he wondered how easy it would be to find plates and forks in the boxes packed away in the basement. The brand-new oak kitchen cabinets hadn't yet been filled with supplies. "I'll scrounge up some plates—"

"I've got some." Val cut him off as she reached for her briefcase on the island. "Your mom is way ahead of you. She sent me with a bunch of supplies. Everything we could need and more." She pulled out plates, silverware, a pie spatula, and cloth napkins. "She tried to send me with candles as well, for ambiance." Val smirked.

"She thinks of everything." Evan shook his head. Maybe it wasn't such a bad thing to have his mom as a matchmaker. At least, not when it came to Val. "We could enjoy the pie next to the firepit, outside? That'd be better ambiance than a few candles."

"Sure." Val's eyes twinkled, making Evan's chest tighten.

"Perfect." He reached for the knife and spatula and cut into the round pie, putting two generous servings on the dessert plates. Gooey apple slices spilled out under the crumbly crust, and Val pulled one more surprise from her briefcase—a glass container. Evan knew what it was before she opened the lid.

"Mom's homemade caramel sauce," he said, adding forks to each plate.

Val hummed in response. "Joyce said to drizzle it on before enjoying." She took a spoonful of the sauce and dripped it over each pie slice in a sweeping zigzag. Evan couldn't help but admire the joy and excitement on her face.

Once the masterpieces were complete, Evan took hold of the plates. "Off to the firepit we go."

Val grabbed the cloth napkins and Skippy followed them out of the house. In the backyard, they walked along the winding stone pathway that Evan had painstakingly laid. It led to a round stone patio, nestled amidst a few birch trees and leafy Hosta plants. At the center of the patio, there was an iron firepit surrounded by cushioned chairs and a cozy bench, beckoning them to take a seat and enjoy the lake view.

"What a perfect spot." Val stopped to take it all in. Skippy trotted around the firepit and sniffed curiously at the woodpile.

"Here," Evan said. "Enjoy your pie. I'll get a fire going for us."

She took both plates with a smile, setting his pie on the bench next to her as she got comfortable. Then she watched Evan stack logs and kindling in the firepit. As the fire started to crackle and illuminate the space, he joined Val on the cushioned bench.

"You're pretty good at that." She slipped a forkful of pie past her pretty lips.

"I've built a fire or two before." He winked. "How's the pie?"

Her eyes fluttered as she practically purred. "I don't think I've ever tasted anything better."

Evan smiled, taking his first bite and joining Val in her delight. Cinnamon, nutmeg, and brown sugar hypnotized his senses. For a few glorious minutes, they stayed silent, enjoying the perfect pie, serene surroundings, and each other's company.

When Valerie ran her fork across the plate, capturing the last bits of syrupy crumbs, she said, "This will *surely* win your mom the blue ribbon."

Evan agreed, licked his lips, and set their empty plates on the ground. Skippy sniffed the air around the dishes, looking like he might sneak a lick when Evan wasn't paying attention. "Mom will be happy to hear that in the morning." He got comfortable next to Val, placing an arm across the top of the bench behind her back. He sighed when she pulled her legs up onto the cushion and cuddled into the crook of his elbow.

She tilted her head toward him. "Am I keeping you from anything?"

Evan chuckled and shook his head. "Only a thrilling Friday night working on purchase orders at the feed store."

She raised a brow. "Work on a Friday night?"

"Figured I might as well get it done." He shrugged, and she grinned.

"Wow. You're as exciting as I am." The flickering flames cast a warm glow, highlighting her smooth olive skin and the curves of her bare legs, exposed by jean shorts. Evan wanted to pull her close, run his hands over her soft skin. Instead, he smiled at Val's teasing comment.

"Hey, I can be exciting when I want to be." He nudged her playfully with his shoulder. "Like when I feel the need to jump in the lake."

Val laughed, the sound musical and carefree. "That was very exciting. I'm glad we did that."

"Me too. And I'm glad you came over tonight." Evan smiled, realizing he could do this every night for eternity and never want for anything else. The thought made him pause, unsure if he should let his mind wind down that path. Was it even a possibility? Shifting his gaze to the fire, he probed the thought cautiously.

"What's the plan after this pilot is done? What's next on the list for Ms. Valerie Ricci?" Surely, she had another project in the works.

Val shifted against the cushions. She wrapped her arms around her knees. "Honestly?"

Her question caught him off guard. "Yes, honestly."

Val stared off, her emerald gaze lost in the fire. "I thought I knew exactly what I wanted." She glanced over at him. "Now I'm not so sure."

The air between them was charged, full of restless energy he couldn't interpret. Evan's heart started pounding. Was she talking about her career, or him? Was she thinking the same thing he was? What it would be like to fall in love again? How their lives could merge into one?

"What do you mean?" he asked, hoping for clarity.

Val traced slow circles on her knees, her expression pensive. Something was bothering her. Evan was about to tell her how much he'd enjoyed spending time with her, and how he was catching feelings he hadn't experienced in a long time, when she spoke up.

"The network is interested in a show Nina and I pitched to them."

Her statement socked Evan right in the gut, and he made a conscious effort not to exhale in defeat. He was dreaming of a future with Val while she was considering her next career move.

"What did you pitch?" He wanted to know her dreams, even if he wasn't part of them.

She eased back against his arm. "A series where I'd travel across America, touring historical buildings and telling their stories." She clasped her hands together in front of her legs. "I thought it was exactly what I wanted."

"But now you don't know if that's what you want?"

Val swallowed and took a breath before speaking. "I'm not good at this."

"Good at what?"

"Being vulnerable." She glanced at him, uncertainty in her eyes. He wanted to ease it away. "I'm good at putting a plan in place and following through with it. I'm *really* good at putting a smile on my face and pretending everything is okay. But I'm not so good at talking about my feelings."

Dropping his hand to her shoulder, he gave her a squeeze. "I'm here to listen, Val. You can tell me whatever you want to. I understand how hard it is to be vulnerable." Heck, when was the last time he'd opened up to a woman? At least, in a romantic sense.

She scanned his face, latching onto his words. "Being here, working on your house, it's reminded me how much I enjoy the creative process. Somehow, I forgot that. But I really do like to swing a hammer, paint walls, and pick out every detail of a house until it becomes a home."

"You're really talented, Val."

"Thanks." She fixed her gaze on the orange flames as they licked up the logs. "But that's not the only thing I've remembered since I've been here." A gentle breeze tossed a strand of hair across Val's face. He reached out and brushed it behind her ear. "You've reminded me what it's like to be seen." She looked at him, affection glazing her eyes.

"Seen?"

"You make me feel important just for being me." She laid her head back, resting it on his arm. "Not for what I've accomplished or because I'm on TV."

His heart twisted at her confession, not understanding how or why anyone would make her feel otherwise. "You deserve to feel that all the time."

"I guess what I'm trying to say is that I've really enjoyed spending this week with you." She reached over and took his hand.

"Me too." Evan's heart surged with hope. Leaning in, he pulled her close, wanting to ask if there was a way to make this work. As their lips met, Evan poured all his feelings into their kiss, trying to convey everything he couldn't say with words. The way he felt about her and the desire to make it work, even if it meant dating long distance—because that would mean there would be more moments like this.

Easing back, Evan looked deep into her eyes. He was ready to tell Val that he didn't want to go back to their separate lives, or how it was before she showed up in his living room, giving him the surprise of a lifetime. But the words got stuck in his throat as a clatter of wood and barking snagged his attention and stole the moment.

They both jerked and spun toward the noise. The neatly stacked wood pile was now scattered about, and Skippy was standing amongst the chaos, growling. Until that very second, Evan had never heard Skippy growl, and he quickly scanned the dark for the source of the pup's concern. He sucked in a breath when he found it. Val must've seen the threat at the same time because they both yelled, "No!"

But their warning did not convince Skippy.

The pup lurched for the other side of the scattered wood pile—toward a *very* disgruntled skunk. A bushy black and white body arched in a threat Skippy did not understand.

At least, not until he got sprayed.

Chapter Seventeen

The next day, Valerie stared at the freshly installed wallpaper, appreciating the delicate blue swirls and hints of marigold as they lit up Issy's bedroom. The paisley paper was pure feminine sunshine, matching the warmth streaming in through bare windows.

"What a perfect choice," Valerie said, slinging an arm around Issy and giving her an approving squeeze.

Issy leaned into the one-armed hug. "I love it!" Looking at Valerie, she scrunched her nose in delight.

"We'll hang the sheer curtains and then your bedroom is move-in ready." Valerie grinned, catching Evan's stare as she did. He was leaning against the door frame, arms crossed and a tool belt slung low on his hips. That was enough to make Valerie's heart kick, but the genuine smile on his face gave her chest a double jump.

"You two ready for a break?" Evan asked. "Mom brought freshly baked maple blondie bars."

Issy and Valerie gasped at the same time.

"That sounds like heaven," Valerie breathed.

"I'm getting down there before Sal eats them all," Issy added, wide-eyed. "I'll meet you guys in the kitchen." She gave Valerie one more squeeze before jogging out the door. As her footsteps echoed down the stairs, Valerie caught Evan's gaze and a rush of anticipation shot through her. They were completely alone. No crew, cameras, or watchful eyes.

Evan pushed off the door frame, uncrossing his muscular arms. He walked to her and pulled her close, wrapping her in an embrace and gazing at her like a precious treasure.

Her heart thrummed.

Leaning close to her ear, he whispered, "How long do you think we'll smell like skunk?"

Valerie burst into laughter, and Evan tightened his embrace, making her want to unclip his tool belt. It was the only barrier to having the full expanse of his body against hers.

"I'd guess we're going to stink for a few days," she replied, not caring that she sported the remnants of last night's skunk chase. She was stinky and tired, having stayed up late with Evan scrubbing Skippy clean—or as clean as they could get him—but her heart was full. Even while battling the foul stench of skunk, they'd laughed and joked, enjoying each other's company over soapy bubbles and scrubbing.

"At least we *both* stink." Evan's powder-blue eyes twinkled, and he bit back a smile.

"At least," she agreed, and Evan leaned in. He kissed her, making her toes curl in her boots. The warmth of his embrace and the press of his lips made her want to forget everything else and live in a bubble for eternity—with Evan. She imagined closing the door, locking it, and losing herself in pure bliss.

"You guys are going to miss out on the blondie bars!" Issy's voice carried up from downstairs. "There's only two left!"

Evan pulled back, and they shared a smile.

"We better get down there," Valerie noted, regretfully. "Even though I'd give up a maple blondie bar to keep kissing you."

Evan looked astonished. "That's a serious sacrifice."

"It'd be worth it."

He kissed her again. "Can I see you tonight?"

Butterflies circled in her belly. She nodded. "Another swim in the lake?"

He brushed his fingers along her spine, sending tingles up her back. "Can I take you out to dinner?"

"Dinner?" she whispered, wanting to spin the clock forward to this evening, but Joyce's voice carried up the stairwell, breaking their embrace.

"Sal is going to eat these if you guys don't get down here right this very second!" Joyce called out, half laughing. "I'm fighting him off right now!"

"She's not kidding," Sal shouted.

Val grinned at Evan. "Dinner would be lovely."

They headed downstairs to join the group. Stepping into the kitchen, Valerie said, "Sorry. We were measuring the windows to make sure I ordered the right rods." Her excuse made little sense because the rods were adjustable, but no one questioned her. The crew was distracted by Joyce's baked goods.

"Yep, had to double-check Val's measurements," Evan said, with a mischievous smile that put a hitch in Valerie's step. She nearly tripped over her own feet, but Evan steadied her with a well-placed hand on her lower back.

She cleared her throat and stifled a smile. When Joyce handed her a glazed bar on a napkin, Valerie immediately sank her teeth into the gooey goodness.

"Oh. My. Goodness," Valerie uttered as she chewed. "I don't know what happens in your kitchen, but it's pure magic."

"Thanks, sweetness." Joyce beamed, wearing a flowered apron that said, "happiness is homemade."

Valerie took another bite, thoroughly content for reasons far beyond the sweet treat, but her bliss was interrupted when Nina burst through the front door.

"Hey, Val?" Nina called, looking alarmed. "Can I talk to you? Over here, please?"

Valerie swallowed and abandoned the half-eaten bar on the island, wondering if something was wrong with the furniture delivery. The truck was parked in the driveway, but they hadn't inspected the goods yet. If the order was wrong, they'd need at least another week to get the pieces Valerie had meticulously picked out. But they only had one more day to get the final shots of Evan's house. The camera crew was scheduled for another project back in Los Angeles and there was no time for mistakes.

"What's wrong?" She met Nina near the front door.

"I want you to know I had nothing to do with this," Nina started, her hands in front of her chest. The concern in her statement set Valerie on edge.

"What are you talking about?" Just as Valerie spoke, a familiar male voice shot through the open front door, slicing straight through Valerie.

"Ryker is here," Nina explained.

Valerie thought the floor had disappeared below her. "Are you serious?"

"Completely serious. Wish I wasn't."

Valerie gasped. "Why?"

Nina shook her head. "Tom just called me. My phone literally rang as Ryker was rolling down the driveway. I tried fighting him on it, but—" She stopped as Ryker strode through the door, crushing Valerie's happiness like a sledgehammer to drywall.

"There you are," Ryker announced with the charm of a man used to getting his way. He looked dressed for an awards show—navy suit, crisp white shirt, and hair styled perfectly for the cameras. His assistant shuffled in behind him, phone to his ear and frantically making notes in a thick planner. Chatter from the kitchen squealed to a stop and Ryker waved over Valerie's shoulder like he was addressing paparazzi.

"Hey, folks." He spoke to the kitchen with a pearly white smile. "Ryker Star here for a guest appearance."

Valerie had always hated how he referred to himself in third person, as if he were constantly introducing himself to the world.

"Guest appearance?" She hoped she hadn't heard him correctly. "On my show?"

"Tom set it up. Thought it would be a good plug for my new series releasing this fall." Ryker cocked his head. His hair didn't move. "But I thought you'd be filming when I arrived. I only have today to get this done. Need to be back at the airport in the morning." He glanced around, looking disappointed at the lack of cameras.

"We're on a break." Nina narrowed her eyes at him, crossing one arm over the other. "I'm not sure what you or Tom expected by not giving me any notice of your arrival."

Ryker made a dismissive noise, looking back at Valerie. "Good to see you again. How have you been?"

Valerie nearly choked. Good to see her again? How has she been? The last time she'd seen Ryker, she'd thrown a full plate of spaghetti at his head—after he'd confessed that he'd been cheating on her for more than a year. Then he dragged her through a messy divorce that rocked her mental state and bank account. Had Ryker hit his head on the way here? Gotten a case of amnesia? Valerie's mouth bounced open like the back end of a garbage truck. She was ready to unload a slew of curses except footsteps closed in behind her.

"Mr. Star," Joyce's sweet voice started, "It's so wonderful to meet you. My granddaughter, Issy, and I are big fans of LA Renovations. We watched you and Val since the very first episode and were so sad when it was cancelled." Joyce outstretched her hand and Ryker lit up at the praise. He took her hand and kissed it, making Joyce giggle like a schoolgirl. Issy stood beside her grandma, looking just as dazzled.

Valerie closed her mouth, not wanting to make a scene. She wouldn't do that in front of the Westons. Neither Joyce nor Issy knew the real Ryker, the one that had strung Valerie along for years, showing her that marriage could be an act, just like television. Still, it hurt to see the excitement on their faces at Ryker's appearance.

"Always a pleasure to meet fans," Ryker cooed, releasing Joyce's hand. "It looks like you're close to doing the final reveal of the renovation." He looked around, taking in all the changes Valerie, the Westons, and the crew had worked hard to complete. "Cute."

The four-letter word grated on Valerie, but she swallowed her irritation. *Cute?* Ryker didn't know the difference between wainscoting and shiplap. He'd always been the face and charm of their show. She'd been the brains. Yet he got the credit for their shared success. She'd taken the blame for their failure.

Biting her tongue, she reined in her thoughts, but Evan took the words out of her mouth.

"Cute would not be the word I'd use to describe the renovation." Evan's tight tone caught Valerie's attention, and she glanced back, confirming he was standing right behind her. His shoulders were squared and jaw clenched, like he might football-tackle Ryker. "Evan Weston." He offered his hand and Ryker shook it, though their handshake was nowhere near as ceremonious as the exchange with Joyce. In fact, Valerie thought Ryker winced before Evan let go. That gave her a zing of satisfaction.

"Oh, the cowboy," Ryker said, nodding. "Yeah, that makes sense."

Valerie's blood simmered. Ryker hadn't technically insulted Evan, but the way he was eying him said otherwise.

"What exactly did Tom send you here for?" she asked, working hard to keep her tone even. She didn't want to lose her cool, but honestly . . . what was happening? Ryker was going to swoop in and put his stamp on her project? Why would Tom send him without talking to her first? He was aware they were not on good terms.

"To help you with a project on the house. Something simple. From the looks of it, you're ready to move in furniture. I could hang some art? Mainly, I'm supposed to talk about my new show and create some buzz for the network."

"Buzz?" Valerie tensed, every muscle locking.

"The viewers are dying to see a reunion of Ryker and Valerie. Tom's been talking to me about it for months." Ryker's easy confidence coated his explanation and punched Valerie in the heart. "It'll spike ratings, for your show and mine. It'll be good for us both."

She stopped breathing, realizing why Tom hadn't warned her about Ryker. This was why he'd given her the job. It wasn't about her talent as a host or her creative abilities. The network had orchestrated this whole thing just to surprise her with her ex-husband. She was being reduced to nothing more than a ratings spike.

Her stomach fell, crashing to her toes. With a glance at Ryker, she uttered, "Of course."

Nina looked like she'd just witnessed a car crash, but Ryker continued, oblivious to the pain or tears welling inside Valerie.

"Great." Ryker spun a finger through the air. "Let's get to filming then." He brushed down the front of his suit jacket, and Valerie tried to swallow her embarrassment. But it was too big. She couldn't push it down.

"I need a minute," Valerie said, knowing she needed more than a few measly minutes to pull herself together. Without making eye contact with anyone, she strode out the still-open front door.

Chapter Eighteen

"I'll go talk to her," Evan told Nina, before striding past Ryker, tempering his urge to escort the unexpected visitor out of town. He wasn't sure what was happening, but Val's energy had shifted when her ex-husband appeared, and Evan needed to make sure she was all right. But when Evan stepped onto his front porch, frustration mixed with his worry. Val was speeding off in the UTV, motoring toward the lake. When she disappeared into the trees, Evan went to his truck, hoping he knew where she was going.

On his way to The Carriage House, Evan tried Val's cell. It rang endlessly and went to voicemail, forcing doubt into his head. Did she want him to come after her? Should he give her space? He wasn't sure, but if she wanted to be left alone, he needed to hear that from her lips. Parking at the inn, he made a beeline for Val's room, but caught sight of the UTV. It was near the lake, parked under the willow tree, half hidden. Then he spotted Val—standing on the far edge of the dock, looking out over the water.

He approached quietly, but when he stepped on the dock, his boots clipped against the wood. She turned to look at him.

"Hi," Val said, as though they were casually meeting.

"Hey." He assessed her crossed arms and hunched shoulders. The need to pull her into a hug was strong, but something about her stance told him he shouldn't. "You okay?"

A tear escaped down her cheek, slashing at Evan's heart. Val brushed it away with a swipe of her fingers. "Not really."

He stepped in front of her, placing his hands on her shoulders. "What can I do?" Should he hold her? Go back and throw Ryker out of his house? Punch him square in the nose? "Do you want me to get rid of him?" She just needed to say the word, and he'd erase any problem.

"No." She shook her head, stirring frustration inside him. He wanted to make this right for her.

"Why is he here?"

Val wiped another tear from her cheek. After a few breaths, she straightened and cleared her throat. Her green eyes wavered as she said, "The network sent him."

"And you didn't know?"

She shook her head. "I didn't."

Now he wanted to rip into the network. "Why would they do that?"

She pressed her lips together, her eyes hollowed out. "To make sure this show is a success."

Evan was at a loss for words. Val had put in all the hard work, time, and ideas, creating a beautiful home for him and Issy. She was the one and only star of the show, in his eyes. "But you're the host. You've done all the work. There's no place for Ryker on your show unless you want him to be there."

Val glanced up, offering a sad smile that felt like a consolation prize. "That's not how the network sees it." She hooked a hand on his bicep and Evan steeled his arm, wanting to support her. "All this time, I thought this was my opportunity to get my career back." She laughed dryly and looked out over the lake. "But the network just wanted to use me for a ratings spike, to plug Ryker's show. They probably sent out the press release that resurfaced all the talk of our divorce and that awful picture, just to get a buzz going and do what's best for the network. They didn't take me into account in any of it." Her gaze slid down to his feet.

Evan's chest twisted. "That's horrible." She didn't deserve to be treated like that—ever. Val wasn't a side character in Ryker's world, or a tool to use as the network saw fit. She deserved respect and praise, and he wanted to shake anyone that wouldn't give her that. "I'm sorry, Val."

"You don't have to be sorry." Her gaze found his and the pain in her eyes solidified. Her shoulders stiffened under his grip, and Evan realized she hadn't taken his words the way he'd meant them.

"No one should treat you like that. You deserve the world, Val," he said, wanting to give it to her. "I'll go tell Ryker off right now. He doesn't deserve to be in your presence, and shame on the network for not seeing how fantastic you are. Give me the president's number. I'll call them and tell them what a bunch of idiots they are, and—"

She gripped his arm, interrupting his rant. "You don't have to do that."

"Yes, I do." He needed Val to know how special she was. She should be put on a pedestal every single minute of every single day. He needed her to know that she was loved . . . by him. "I want to."

"I know." She shook her head. "But I got myself into this spot and I need to be the one to get myself out. Please let me do that, okay?"

A wad of feelings lodged in his chest. How could he stand by and watch someone he loved fight a battle alone? He didn't know how to do that. It went against every instinct he had.

"I need to do this myself," she reiterated. The determination in her stare cut him off at the knees. As much as it pained him, he nodded. But his heart broke in a way no surgery could heal.

"Whatever you want."

"Thank you." Val squeezed his arm once more, holding tight before letting her hand slip from his bicep. He released her too, focusing all his energy on keeping his boots in place. It took every ounce of strength he had to watch her walk down the dock and back to the inn.

He didn't chase her. Because he knew she didn't want him to.

Chapter Nineteen

Tears streamed down Valerie's face as she stepped inside The Carriage House. She hastily wiped them away, wishing she could do the same for the emotions stirring inside her. She'd wanted so badly to curl up in Evan's arms, to let him rush in and make her problems disappear. But after everything she'd endured with Ryker, she couldn't allow anyone else to fix her problems. She needed to stand up for herself. She couldn't stay silent while someone else told her story.

Except, did she know her story now?

Should she call Tom and tell him where he could stick his hairbrained idea? Swallow her pride and film with Ryker, just to get the ratings? Did she even want to pursue the show she and Nina had pitched, just to be at the mercy of a network that cared nothing for her? And what was she supposed to do with all the feelings she had for Evan?

Valerie paused as she entered her room, the last question hitting her hard—which was frightening. Love had never worked out for her in the past. Placing her trust in a man had only brought heartache. But her work had always been there for her—a constant and rewarding companion. Or so she'd thought.

Overwhelmed, Valerie reached for the first thing she thought of to ease her worries—her suitcase. Tomorrow evening she'd be on a plane, and she needed to pack. Flipping her suitcase open on the bed, she started gathering her things, seeking comfort in structure and organization.

As she folded and arranged each piece of clothing, Valerie focused on the process of packing. She wanted to bring order to her life just like she was doing with her suitcase, but it wasn't that simple.

While in Maple Bay, Valerie had gained more than she'd expected. She'd arrived with a suitcase full of dress clothes and high heels. But now her designer clothes were mixed with Wranglers and T-shirts. She even owned a baseball hat. The person she thought she was, and the plan she'd meticulously mapped out, had been mixed up and rewritten in one short week. Not to mention, with all the new purchases, her bag was overflowing. So when Valerie reached for her cowboy boots—the fancy pair she and Issy had fawned over—there was no room left for them.

Her heart shattered into a million pieces.

It wasn't about the boots or the clothes. Her heart was breaking for the special people and memories they represented. How had she fallen for Evan and his family in a matter of days?

Placing her hands on the edge of her suitcase, tears rolled out, escaping into folded clothes. The overstuffed bag was a jumble of feelings and memories she didn't know how to sort through. She *was* her suitcase, trying to combine an old life with a new one and realizing something had to give. Otherwise, her zipper was going to burst.

Looking down at the half-folded mess, a slideshow played through her head. The ice cream date. The dip in the lake she'd never forget. Her first supper with his family. All the laughter and smiles she and Evan had shared while breaking down walls and patching holes—in his house and in her heart.

Was this love? Was true love staring her in the face, and she was panicking?

Maybe. Possibly... Yes.

Valerie sighed at herself. What was she running from? Happiness?

Somehow, in a single week, Evan had reminded her of who she was and what she deserved. She'd healed, grown, and smiled more than she'd ever expected, and as her tears dried, Valerie knew what she wanted.

And what she didn't.

Turning from her suitcase, she walked to the sink and splashed cold water on her face, washing away the last of her lingering doubts. She was ready to tell her story, the full truth, even though it would burn bridges.

Chapter Twenty

Evan sought refuge in the barn, hoping to clear his head, but visions of Valerie's sad eyes sucked up every single thought. He fought the pull to go after her, but it took every ounce of his energy to do so. When he absentmindedly left a stall door wide open and Pistol trotted down the aisle, Jesse intervened, grabbing hold of the colt.

"Hey, you okay?" Jesse asked, guiding the horse back into his stall. "You seem off."

Evan rubbed a hand over his forehead. "Sorry. That was my fault."

Kat strode past Evan and dumped a scoop of grain in Pistol's feeder. The colt dug in, forgetting his romp. "Yeah, you never do stuff like that. You sick or something? You're white as a ghost."

Sick? *Yes*. His stomach was turning, but it had nothing to do with a bug or virus.

"Yeah, maybe." He didn't want to spill the real reason he wasn't feeling like himself. Eventually, he'd tell his brother and sister, but right now he was just trying to keep his head on straight. He wouldn't vomit up his feelings. Not while they were battling inside him. He needed to sift through the rubble first.

"We got this." Jesse furrowed his brow as he assessed Evan. "Go lay down or something. No need to be out here working if you're not feeling well."

"Jesse and I can feed." Kat closed the stall door. "You definitely need to go lay down." Not waiting for an answer, she took Evan's arm and turned him toward the door. "Go, now. I'm calling Mom and telling her you're on your way with strict instructions to get comfortable on the couch."

Normally, Evan would've fought such orders, but he couldn't muster up the energy. "Okay," he uttered, thinking he could use a minute to recoup.

Kat gave him a comforting pat on the back. "Feel better soon. We'll check on you after we take care of the horses."

Walking out of the barn, Evan hoped to feel better, but he didn't know how to shake the unease in his gut—other than to pull Val close and confess his love for her. But he'd been burned in the past, giving his heart to the wrong person or at the wrong time, and that included Val. Would she return his feelings now? Could he risk another heartbreak?

Questions riddled his head as he opened the door and entered his parents' kitchen. His mom was near the oven, apron on and phone to her ear. Three freshly baked pies sat on the island, filling the house with warmth and sweetness. Usually, just the thought of his mom's baking would make his mouth water, but he had no appetite.

"Okay. Thanks, sweetie. Love you," his mom said into the phone before setting it on the counter. Her solemn face told Evan she'd been talking to Kat.

"I'm okay, Mom," he said, but the worry etched on her face sent a shot of guilt through him.

"You don't look okay." She took off her apron and set it aside. Ever since his heart surgery, she'd been extra sensitive to his health, and he could feel her anxiety creeping in.

"I'm fine," he reiterated. "I'm just going to sit down for a minute."

His mom strode to the table and pulled out a chair, gesturing for him to take a seat. "Do you feel faint?"

"No." He sat down.

"Nauseous?" His delayed answer caused her to continue. "Shortness of breath?"

"No."

"Chest pain?" She placed a hand on the back of a chair, steadying herself, and Evan's insides buckled.

"It's not my heart, Mom." Placing an arm on the table, the irony in his statement hit him. There *was* a problem with his heart, but not in the way she thought.

"Good golly. What's going on then? You're going to give *me* a heart attack."

Seeing his mom's face, Evan knew one thing. He needed to tell her the truth. He'd been carrying his secret for far too long. "Mom, can you sit? There's something I need to tell you."

The chair squealed across the floor. His mom took a seat, facing him. "What is it, child? Tell me." She put a hand on his knee, and Evan felt a surge of gratitude for her unwavering support. His mom had always been there for him and their family, ready to lend a helping hand at a moment's notice.

"Do you remember the woman I dated my senior year of college?" he asked, leaning into the solid oak table.

Her forehead creased in thought. "Who?"

"Valerie Ricci. We dated long-distance. She went to the University of Nebraska."

Recognition eased into her eyes. "Oh, yes. I remember. You told me so much about her." She squinted. "But why are we talking about an old college flame?"

"Because she came back into my life this past week." A mix of anxiety and relief coursed through him. "In a very unexpected and wonderful way. In fact, I came home one evening, and she was standing in my living room next to you and Issy."

"What are you—" His mom froze, like she'd discovered a hornet in her pie. "Are you saying that *our* Ms. Valerie Star and *your* college flame are the same person?"

He nodded.

His mom gasped, a hand flying to her mouth. "Evan!" Her eyes were the size of tractor wheels.

He cringed, but didn't falter. "That's not all." Leaning forward, he placed a hand over his mom's, taking in her warmth. "Val and I were engaged. Twenty years ago, I proposed to her."

His mom's hand tightened on his knee like a vice-grip. "You proposed? To Val?"

"I did. And she said yes." His chest squeezed. "But two days later, she gave me back the ring and called off the engagement. I was crushed and embarrassed, but now I understand why she left. In a strange way, I'm thankful we broke up. We weren't ready for marriage then."

His mom blinked. Her mouth hung open.

"I'm sorry I didn't tell you," Evan started, recalling every missed opportunity he'd had to share his secret. "I was hurt. Back then I was too embarrassed to tell you or dad. I just wanted to forget it happened."

His mom's shoulders squared, but a moment later, she relaxed. "I wish you'd told me." She sighed.

"I should have."

"Your dad and I are here for you, no matter what. I hope you know that."

"I do." Evan offered a sincerely remorseful smile. "I should've told you sooner."

The kitchen was quiet, except for the tick of the clock above the sink. "Like when your daughter and I were binge watching seasons of LA Renovations? Or gossiping about Valerie and Ryker's divorce? Or when I surprised you with your ex-fiancé and a reality show?" His mom shocked him with a laugh. "Goodness gracious, Evan. Why didn't you stop me?"

For a second, Evan was shocked. Then relief washed over him, and he let out a breathy chuckle. "To be honest, now I'm not sure."

She shook her head. "Well, I'm glad you didn't."

"You are?" he asked, confused by the turn of their conversation.

"Yes." She patted his hand. "Because if I'd known, Val wouldn't be here now. I wouldn't have let that happen. And I can tell there's something special between the two of you."

Straightening, he asked, "How can you tell?" He'd been hiding his feelings for Val this entire week, but he'd apparently done a crummy job.

"She makes you happy," his mom said matter-of-factly. "I see it in the way you light up around her. You practically glow."

Evan nodded, taking in his mom's words. They perfectly captured how he felt. Val made his heart happy, filling each day with warmth and sunshine. "I think I love her."

His mom gasped and squeezed his hand with both of hers. "You love Val?"

"I think I do," he reiterated, even though he absolutely knew that he loved Val. He just couldn't bring himself to say it aloud. Not yet.

"Listen to your heart. You know that little voice inside you? It says big things. Don't ignore it."

Evan simply nodded. His mom was right. That little voice inside him was nearly shouting.

Just then, the back door opened, and Issy strode into the kitchen. Skippy plodded along at her heels. "Oh, it smells good in here," she announced, her gaze finding the pies and then sliding to Evan and his mom. Her forehead creased in confusion. "What are you guys doing?"

Evan clenched up, not ready to have the same conversation with his daughter, but his mom didn't miss a beat.

"Talking about life and baking." His mom patted his hand and stood up. "Do you want a piece of maple sugar cream pie?" she asked Issy, effectively distracting her with the lure of baked goods.

"Um, yes." Issy put her hands on the island and stared down at the pies. "Have I ever said no to your baking?"

As his mom and Issy chatted about pie and the upcoming Sunday supper, Evan sat at the kitchen table, lost in thought. His mom always knew just what to say, and this time was no exception. Instead of being upset that he'd kept information from her, she'd urged him to listen to his heart. And his heart was telling him to confess the depth of his feelings to Val, no matter what she had to say in return. The way he felt about her was a secret he couldn't keep any longer.

"Dad, are you going to have some pie?" Issy asked, breaking through his thoughts.

Evan rose from the chair. "Actually, can you guys save me a piece for later? I promised Val I'd take her out to dinner tonight."

Issy gave him a strange look before putting a forkful of pie in her mouth. "Really?"

Evan's stomach sank. "Yeah, you good with that?" Would Issy have a problem with Evan taking Val on a date? Because that would flip everything he'd considered right on its head.

"I'm totally good with it." She looked at him like he'd just asked her if she was going to have more pie. "If you haven't noticed, Grandma and I have been trying to get you and Val together all week. We love her."

His mom smiled and shrugged. "We do."

Evan grinned ear to ear. Warmth and certainty spread through him, solidifying his decision.

"Val was amazing on TV, but she's a million times more amazing in person," Issy added, wiping her mouth with a napkin. "But I saw Val and Nina driving toward town about twenty minutes ago. Are you *sure* you asked her to go out to dinner tonight?"

Evan gave Issy a kiss on her forehead. "Don't you worry about it. I'll get it figured out." After hugging both Issy and his mom, he headed outside. In the warm evening air, he typed up a text and sent it to Val. Then Evan drove to his house to wait.

Chapter Twenty-one

Once in town, Valerie and Nina found an adorable candy shop, bought a pound of truffles, and took the sweet treats to a picnic table by the lake.

As soon as they sat down, Nina said, "I can't believe Tom sent your ex to our set." Nina shook her head adamantly. Pausing, she held up a finger. "Actually, I take that back. I'm not sure why that surprised either of us. Tom is a complete jerk." She called him a few more four-letter words before opening the box of chocolates and offering them to Valerie.

"He absolutely is." Valerie agreed wholeheartedly, plucking out a dusted dark chocolate truffle. "And I can't wait to tell him so. I've worked too hard for HomeTV to be treated like I'm disposable."

"Amen, sister."

Valerie popped the sweet into her mouth, contemplating the past few hours as she chewed. She'd been through a rollercoaster of emotions, but had also gotten a lot of clarity. "The network doesn't see my worth, and they don't get to decide what happens with my career. Not anymore. Those choices belong to me." With a deep exhale, tension began draining from her body.

Nina nodded before wiping her mouth with a napkin. "So, you're going to call Tom, but I get to break the news to Ryker?" Her eyes twinkled with delight and mischief.

"Sounds like a deal to me. I've had enough Ryker to last me a lifetime. I'm happy to let you handle him."

Nina grinned, rubbing her hands together like a cartoon villain. "I can't wait to see his face when I tell him he's not allowed on my set." She looked like she might cackle, which coaxed a smirk from Valerie.

"He'll definitely be surprised." Valerie didn't wish Ryker ill-will, but she also wouldn't let him mess with her life or make decisions for her. Never again.

"He can take his surprise *and* his smug, good-for-nothing ego right back to the airport." Nina tossed a hazelnut praline truffle in her mouth and chewed in delight.

"He was very concerned about getting back to the airport quickly."

"It's a win-win for everyone."

Valerie leaned on the picnic table. "We'll do the makeover reveal tomorrow, wrap up filming, and complete our contracts."

"Exactly. Then you and I decide what comes next."

Valerie smiled, elated at how things were falling into place. "Thank goodness we have an amazing agent."

"She's the best."

Nina and Valerie's entertainment agent was a whiz with contracts and negotiations. They'd called her before heading into town, and she'd confirmed they were legally obligated to finish filming the pilot. But after that, they could walk away. Their contracts stated that any significant changes to the show's concept would require a new agreement. And Ryker's involvement was a significant change. Tom would have to find a new host and producer to complete the series.

"I'm really excited for what's next." Valerie reached out and put a hand on Nina's arm. "I know you're not the warm-and-fuzzy type, but I'm so thankful to have a friend like you." Knowing that Nina had her back added to Valerie's comfort and confidence. They'd already discussed pitching their idea for the historical architectural tours to a different network, streaming service, or even funding the project themselves. They'd create something extraordinary together, especially with complete creative control. Above all, she cherished having a loyal and dependable friend at her side.

Nina blushed at Valerie's words, looking touched and uncomfortable at the same time. "Same here," she said, before sliding the box of chocolates toward Valerie. "The last lavender honey truffle is for you."

Valerie grinned. That was Nina's way of showing how much she cared. "Thanks." She popped the chocolate into her mouth and savored the sweet and floral notes. However, uncertainty quickly snuck its way into her head. There was another crucial conversation she needed to tackle. After finishing the treat, Valerie confessed, "I have feelings for Evan, but I might've messed everything up."

Nina raised her brows, though she didn't look confused. "Why do you think you screwed it up?"

Valerie clasped her hands together. "He came to talk to me after the Ryker incident, asking what he could do to help, but I pushed him away. I wanted to handle things on my own."

"And you did," Nina said swiftly, dismissing her concern. "You figured out what you wanted and you're making it happen. Why can't you do that with Evan, too?"

The question pinged around in Valerie's head like her brain was playing tennis. "I think I'm just . . . scared?"

"Of what?"

Valerie swallowed. "Love? Heartbreak?"

"You act as if they're the same." Nina's expression was smooth and serious. "You can have one without the other. Love and heartbreak don't have to be intertwined."

Her words hit a chord deep in Valerie's chest, clearing the fog before her. Had she been using her fear of heartbreak as an excuse to avoid love?

"You know what? You're right." The knot in Valerie's chest unraveled. "I need to tell Evan how I feel about him."

Nina bobbed her head. "Yes, you do. And if for some crazy reason it doesn't work out, you'll deal with it. You're a heck of a lot stronger than you think. And I'll be here for you no matter what."

Warmth circled Valerie. "Thanks, Nina. You're the best."

Nina waved her off. "Just doing my job as your friend." She winked. "Now, let's get back to the van so I can drive you to your cowboy and you guys can ride off into the sunset together."

Valerie stood from the picnic table, a newfound excitement growing inside her. She was ready to take the plunge and spill her guts to Evan. To *her* cowboy. It wouldn't be easy, but it'd be worth it. Pulling her phone from her purse, Valerie prepared to call Evan and ask him to meet up. However, he was one step ahead of her.

Evan: Still want to have dinner with me? My place? Take as long as you need. No rush. I'll wait as long as it takes.

Her heart swelling, Valerie stuffed her phone back in her purse and looked at Nina. "How fast can you drive?"

Chapter Twenty-two

Valerie hopped out of the van and ran toward Evan's house, hoping she wasn't too late. But her heart fell when she opened the front door. It was dark and empty. Checking her phone, Valerie confirmed there were no new messages from Evan, and just as she was about to call him, a faint glow in the backyard caught her eye. Hope spread through her chest, and she strode through the house. Yanking opened the backdoor, she stopped in her tracks.

Evan's red Chevy truck was parked near the willow tree, its bed transformed into a cozy sanctuary filled with pillows and blankets. Two overturned wooden milk cartons served as tables, set with plates, silverware, and flickering candles. Her breath hitched at the romantic gesture, but fireworks exploded in her belly when her gaze landed on Evan. He was near the shed, sanding a porch swing balanced on sawhorses. As she walked toward him, his gaze slid to hers and the smile that followed nearly pushed her into a run.

"Am I too late for dinner?" she asked, barely controlling her urge to leap into his arms.

Releasing the sandpaper, Evan shook his head. "You're never too late."

Goosebumps prickled her arms, his words resonating in so many ways. "I was hoping you'd say that."

"But I hope you're okay with pizza." He stood and dusted his hands off on his jeans. "I picked up a sausage, black olive, and red onion deep dish from Jake's. It should still be warm, but if it's not, I've got this fancy new oven we can heat it up in."

"Perfect." She stepped close, setting a hand on the partially sanded wooden swing. "You're going to refinish the porch swing after all?" He'd seemed so resistant to the idea earlier that week.

Evan took her hand, threading their fingers together. "My grandpa made this swing for my grandma when they were first married." Their hands settled on the swing and Valerie felt a rush of warmth, as if love itself radiated from the wooden slats.

"That's really special," she whispered.

"They sat on it together every chance they got." His eyes lit up at the memory. "I can still picture them holding hands, talking, and enjoying each other's company. To me, this swing symbolizes everything I want in life."

Pushing past the swelling lump in her throat, Valerie asked, "You want someone to sit on the swing with you?"

"Not just anyone." He guided their intertwined hands to his chest, placing them on his heart. It beat against the back of her hand. "I want to share this swing with you. I want us to refinish it, blending the past with the present. From this moment forward, I want to spend every minute building a great love with you. Every single day." His heart thumped intently, as if it were beating for the both of them. "If you'll let me."

Valerie pressed her lips together, her eyes brimming with joyful tears. As she struggled to find the words to express her overwhelmed emotions, Evan added, "But I also need you to know I won't keep you from your dreams." His powder-blue eyes gave her a jolt, cementing her feelings for him. "I know how important your career is to you, and I would never keep you from anything that makes you happy. I want to be with you in whatever way works for us. If that means dating long-distance, then so be it. I want to make this . . . *us* . . . work in whatever way I can."

Valerie couldn't hold back a tear. It raced down her cheek. "I want that too." She wasn't sure her response was coherent, but Evan's genuine smile told her he understood. After clearing her throat, she continued. "In the past week, you've opened my eyes and my heart because you allowed me to be myself."

He ran his thumb across her cheek, wiping away the rogue tear. "I wouldn't have it any other way."

She leaned into his touch. "You gave me the support and space I needed to remember who I am and what I truly want. Today, I decided I won't be continuing with HomeTV after this pilot is complete."

Evan blinked rapidly. "You did?"

She gave a curt nod. "I want to pave my own path, instead of always bending to the network's ideas and standards." She took a deep breath, steadying her emotions. "But more importantly, I want to build something great with you. I can see us sitting on this swing, under the stars, talking about our dreams and the future." She squeezed his hand, relishing the warmth of his skin against hers. "I love you, Evan Weston," she declared, the truth settling deep in her heart. "I love you and your family, and I can't imagine my life without you."

Evan's chest rose with a quick breath, and everything around them disappeared. He pulled her close and kissed her with a conviction that left her breathless, conveying through every touch that he was committing to her.

"I love you, too," he whispered, his arms wrapped tightly around her, grounding her in a way she never thought possible. "Val, I know you came here to fix my house, but you've done one heck of a makeover on my heart."

Her smile widened, grateful for each step that had brought her to this moment.

"Best renovation ever," she replied with a kiss.

She'd discovered the true definition of home—a place built and supported by love. And in Evan's embrace, she knew *this* was what home should feel like.

Epilogue

ONE YEAR LATER

Anxiously, Evan stood in his backyard, the lake shimmering behind him. Jesse and Creed were at his side, decked out in suits and cowboy hats, supporting him on a day he'd never forget. Before him, all his family and friends sat on rows of hay bales, chatting softly. When music filled the air, everyone's attention went to the willow tree—where Val and her bridesmaids awaited, hidden beneath wispy branches.

First to appear was Issy, radiating a smile that could move mountains. Evan's heart swelled with pride as he watched his daughter, adorned in a pale blue dress, walk down the grassy aisle with grace and confidence. He couldn't get over the woman she'd become—kind, brilliant, and ready to conquer the world. In a few short months, she'd start a new chapter in California, having earned a full scholarship to the esteemed school of arts and architecture at UCLA. She'd be across the country, but Evan couldn't be happier for her. She was chasing her dreams and finding her own way. And the second she needed anything, he'd be there for her. Always.

As Issy reached him, Evan pulled her into a warm embrace, unable to hold back a tear.

"I love you, Daddy." She kissed him on the cheek.

"Love you too, sweetie."

"You're going to flip when you see her." She beamed and Evan chuckled, loving how Issy had been so excited about and involved with the wedding plans. She and Val had become quite the adorable pair, having their own special bond.

As Issy took her spot, Jesse's little girl, Charlie, started down the aisle. The sight of Charlie merrily walking alongside the furry ring bearer, Skippy, instigated a murmur of laughter from the crowd. Holding a basket of flowers in one hand and Skippy's leash in the other, Charlie romped down the aisle. Skippy, blissfully unaware of his role, happily wagged his tail and greeted guests, even stealing a few licks along the way.

When the cute duo reached Evan, he affectionately patted them both on the head before Jesse stepped in. He directed his daughter toward Hazel, who sat in the front row, and deftly untied the rings from Skippy's collar. Then the melody shifted, and Evan's heart bounded as he eagerly awaited his bride. Through the gently swaying willow branches, he caught glimpses of Val's white silhouette. When her sister Gigi pulled the branches aside, Evan thought the earth rumbled. Val stepped out, a vision from a fairytale. His fairytale.

White lace skimmed her hourglass figure, accentuating her timeless beauty. Dark curls cascaded over bare shoulders and a delicate veil danced in the breeze.

Evan's gaze locked with hers. A mixture of awe and gratitude flooded his chest. How had he been so lucky as to love this woman twice in one lifetime?

Gigi took Val's arm, ready to walk her sister down the aisle. They shared an intimate moment and a few whispers before falling into step with the music. As Val floated toward him, Evan found himself at a loss for words. Nothing could accurately describe the magnitude of emotions swelling in his chest.

When Val reached him, Gigi took her bouquet and hugged her sister. Then Gigi turned to Evan and said, "I love you guys so much and I'm so happy to call you my brother." Joyful tears filled her eyes. "The only thing I ask is that you both come visit me as much as possible in Chicago."

"Deal." Evan hugged his new sister-in-law. "And you're welcome here anytime. We have a big house with a perfectly decorated guest room. You're family. You don't need to call. Just show up."

Gigi squeezed him back before stepping away and going to stand next to Issy. Then it was just Evan and his stunning bride-to-be.

"Hey, cowboy," Val said, with a smile that lassoed him.

He took her hand. "Hey, cowgirl." He grinned at the pet names they'd given each other. Val may have spent a good portion of her life in Los Angeles, but she had the spirit of a cowgirl. She continuously dazzled him with her gumption.

In the past year, she'd pitched and started her own reality show with a popular streaming service. She and Nina had then produced a limited series showcasing historical buildings, which they'd filmed in less than a month. They already had a contract for season two. Val had also sold her condo in L.A. and started her own home renovation business based in Maple Bay. Initially, she stayed at The Carriage House. After Evan got down on one knee, Val moved in with him, completing his home.

Now they started every morning with coffee and kisses. Every evening ended together on the porch swing. Soon, he could call her Mrs. Weston.

"Are you ready?" the officiant asked, referring to the ceremony, but today symbolized so much more than a wedding. It was about love, commitment, and a lifetime together.

Evan squeezed Val's hand. "I'm ready for now, forever, and always. No matter what life throws at us, I want to do it together."

"Me too," Val replied, her eyes sparkling with certainty.

Evan smiled, marveling at the resilience of the human heart. It could be mended and healed. And his mended heart belonged to Val.

Sincerely Not Yours

WANT TO READ GIGI'S SWEET LOVE STORY?

Get *Sincerely Not Yours* Today!
She's full of holiday cheer. He's the grinch stealing her joy. Tis the season for falling in love.

Stay in touch & never miss a new release ~ Sign-up for Brittney Joy's newsletter:
http://www.brittneyjoybooks.com/newsletter

Thank You

Thank you for reading *Matched in Maple Bay*! I hope this story touched your heart the way it touched mine. If you enjoyed it, I'd love it if you would post your honest review anywhere you purchased your book. Reviews help me understand what stories readers enjoy. They also help me decide what to write next. Your review is greatly appreciated! And if you loved it, tell your friends! The best way to spread the word about a book is through word of mouth!

Never miss a new release ~ Join Brittney Joy's newsletter:
http://www.brittneyjoybooks.com/newsletter

Recipe: Joyce's Caramel Apple Pie

Filling:

 1 cup sugar

 ¼ cup all purpose flour

 1 tsp cinnamon

 6 cups apples, peeled & chopped

 ½ cup caramel sauce

 2 tbsp milk

Crust:

1 cup all-purpose flour

½ cup brown sugar

½ cup butter

 1. Filling: in a large bowl, mix 1 cup sugar, ¼ cup flour, &

cinnamon. Add apples & toss to coat. Combine the milk & 2 tbsp caramel & drizzle over the apples.

2. "Crust" (this will be more like a crumbly crisp crust): in a second bowl, combine 1 cup flour and ½ cup brown sugar. Cut in ½ cup butter until the mixture resembles coarse crumbs.

3. In a greased pie plate, put half of the "crust" in a loose layer. Add the apple mixture on top. Add rest of "crust" as a top layer.

4. Cover the edges of the pie with foil and put pie on a baking sheet.

5. Bake at 350 degrees for 30 minutes. Remove foil. Bake another 25-30 minutes.

6. Cool 15 minutes. Cut, serve, and drizzle with the remaining caramel sauce.

7. Enjoy with family & friends!

Author's Note

The caramel apple pie recipe I have included in this book is one I've lovingly tweaked over the years. It's one of my husband and kids' favorites and I bake quite a few of these in the fall. My family and I live in the country, and we have a small orchard with about ten fruit trees, including apple, pear, and plum trees. Most of the trees are apple and I love it when they are so full of fruit that I can easily pluck big, juicy apples from their branches. I'm always looking for ways to use the fruit and this recipe has become a staple. I often make a bunch of these pies in disposable tin foil pie pans and freeze them to give as gifts. If you'd like to do this, you don't need to bake the pies. Prepare them just as the recipe says, but instead of baking, cover the top tightly in two layers of tin foil, and freeze. I like to write instructions on how to bake on the tin foil with a sharpie.

In *Starting Over in Maple Bay* (book 1), Hazel mentions that baking is her love language. This is one hundred percent me. If I take the time to bake you a treat, it is because I love and care about you and want to see you smile. Sharing my recipes with you throughout the Maple Bay series is my way of sharing a piece of my heart with you. With my baking and my stories, my wish is that they make you smile and warm your heart.

Enjoy and take care,
Brittney

Also by Brittney Joy

Sweet Romance Books:
Rescued in Maple Bay
Starting Over in Maple Bay
Second Chance in Maple Bay
Country Stars in Maple Bay
Matched in Maple Bay
Christmas in Silver Leaf Falls
Sincerely Not Yours

Red Rock Ranch Series: Young Adult Contemporary
Lucy's Chance
Showdown
Rodeo Daze

The OverRuled Series: Young Adult Fantasy
OverRuled
OverRun
OverThrown

Checkout all books here:

www.brittneyjoybooks.com

About the Author

Brittney Joy writes sweet stories full of hope, heart, and happily-ever-afters. She and her family live in their own piece of heaven in the Oregon countryside. They stay busy with their menagerie of silly horses, cackling chickens, wooly sheep, two very naughty goats, a scheming cat, and an adorable dog. When Brittney isn't writing, she's riding or reading. And she wishes she could do all three at the same time.

www.brittneyjoybooks.com

www.ingramcontent.com/pod-product-compliance
Lightning Source LLC
Chambersburg PA
CBHW022136240626
47153CB00007B/2381